South Phoenix Rules

Books by Jon Talton

The David Mapstone Mysteries:
Concrete Desert
Cactus Heart
Camelback Falls
Dry Heat
Arizona Dreams
South Phoenix Rules

The Cincinnati Casebooks:
The Pain Nurse

Other Novels
Deadline Man

South Phoenix Rules

A David Mapstone Mystery

Jon Talton

Poisoned Pen Press

Copyright © 2010 by Jon Talton

First Edition 2010

10 9 8 7 6 5 4 3 2 1

Library of Congress Catalog Card Number: 2010923861

ISBN: 9781590588147   Hardcover
       9781590588161   Trade Paperback

Poisoned Pen Press
6962 E. First Ave., Ste. 103
Scottsdale, AZ 85251
www.poisonedpenpress.com
info@poisonedpenpress.com

Printed in the United States of America

For Susan

Prologue

The August heat in Phoenix has a color. It is not red or orange or any searing hue that could be imagined by you or me or Dante, even though this earthly inferno clocked in that day at one hundred fourteen degrees, the reading on a thermometer safely in the shade at Sky Harbor International Airport and the temperature reported across the radio by announcers sitting in air-conditioned studios. On the pavement, under the midday sun in a city where we all longed for the night, a ground temperature sensor would show one hundred forty degrees, and the cloudless sky was the color of bleached concrete.

It had been a dreadful summer, another record-breaker, and that was before one of the two gasoline pipelines that feeds the autopia that is America's fifth most populous city ruptured. The fireball that consumed the errant backhoe and its operator was only the start of the trouble. Gas stations ran dry. People started classic hoarding behavior, topping off their tanks any time they saw a station with supplies. It made the shortages worse. The newspaper carried stories about price gouging. It reminded me of an article I had read, saying that MI5, Britain's security agency, has a maxim that society is "four meals away from anarchy." This was especially true in a city so dependent on driving, so isolated, so based on complex systems in such an unnatural place to sustain four million people. A vibe of barely contained panic could be felt.

By the second week of the interruption, people followed tanker trucks, hoping they carried a full load and were on their way to a filling station. The county was stockpiling gasoline for uniformed units. Guys like me, we had our county credit cards. We had to do the best we could—with the rule that we had to return the vehicle on full. I wish the deputy who drove the car before me had been so mindful of the regs. The fuel gauge of my unmarked Ford Crown Victoria showed an eighth of a tank.

That day I seemed lucky as I drove out of Maryvale on Thomas Road, headed downtown. Half a block ahead, I saw a long tanker turn left into a gas station. I pulled in behind the truck, landing third in line for one set of pumps, although not close enough to get the shade of the overhang. The plastic bottle of water that had been frozen at nine a.m.—Lindsey and I kept a dozen in the freezer along with the gin during the summer months—was now completely thawed, yet was still cool. I took a last swig.

It was a typical corner station and mini-mart, a squared-off building along a wide avenue of other homely boxes. Twelve lanes crossed the intersection. Two other corners had abandoned gas stations, their remains fenced in. The fourth corner held a check-cashing outlet. Campaign signs clustered on each corner, including one of the wide Peralta Sheriff signs he had been using every election. Peralta was in white, along with a white star, against a blue and red field. Next to it was a sign for his primary opponent, with the subtitle: Stop illegal immigration! The primary would come and go, but the immigrants would come, no matter the condition of the economy. How many had died in the desert this year? Last count: one hundred twenty. None of the Anglos in Phoenix took notice.

At the gas station, the cars quickly lined up, then spilled out onto Thomas. Horns honked. Nobody ever used to honk in Phoenix.

A white Dodge van edged up behind me. Inside were a pretty Anglo mom and a little girl with curly hair. They were in the wrong part of town, but, hey, I was a cop. They'd be safe. My gaze lingered in the rearview mirror and I smiled.

It took away the nastiness of the morning, where I had backed up a uniformed deputy as we evicted a family from their home. The scruffy lawn ended up littered with furniture, clothes, and brightly colored children's toys as we looked on. It's not my job. I was officially the historian of the Maricopa County Sheriff's Office, but I'm also a sworn deputy. Everybody's work had changed since the real-estate crash sent the local economy into a depression. Anyone could have seen it coming, anyone except the majority of Phoenicians who made their living off the growth machine. A columnist in the *Arizona Republic* repeatedly warned it was unsustainable; he was pushed out of a job. Even law enforcement was a victim of the worst government budget cuts in the state's history. So Peralta made me work uniformed shifts, serve warrants, and now throw a family out of its house. My pile of cold cases grew higher. "They can wait," he said.

So I sat there, sweating even though the air conditioning was on high, and smiled at the mother and her little girl waiting behind me.

Then the gun fell.

It clattered to the cement loud enough to be heard inside the car. I made it for a Glock 17, black and blocky, just like many cops carry. My pulse shot, making my temples throb. My hand automatically went to the Colt Python .357 magnum in the Galco high-ride leather holster on my belt.

The kid reached down and picked it up as if nothing more than a crescent wrench had fallen out of his pocket. He slid it into the waistband of his jeans at the small of his back and covered it with his T-shirt. He was maybe twenty, Hispanic, with close-cropped black hair and long limbs. His arms were black with tattoos, and he had bracelets on one wrist. He also had four friends. They were in the car ahead of me, a tricked-out, low Honda. I wondered how they all had fit inside. In front was a blue Chrysler PT Cruiser with another four Hispanic men. One was tall, his muscles showing out of a white wife-beater, the back of his shaved head bearing an elaborate tattoo with two large ornate letters and a line of script below it. This was gang territory and I had parked right in the middle of a meeting. They stood agitated around the cars, brassy *banda* music loudly pouring out of the Cruiser. They were waiting for the gas to flow.

I snapped the holster secure and decided to let things be. Maryvale, Scaryvale. The onetime suburban dream had turned to linear slum and the daily shootings usually didn't even make the newspaper. The tanker driver slid down out of his cab. He set out orange traffic cones around the massive two-trailer rig. I tried not to imagine a scenario where it exploded here. Next, he slid on thick gloves and used a hand-held bar to remove the heavy steel covers embedded in the concrete that led to the underground storage tanks. They clanged loudly. After pulling out a long pole to measure the tanks—a pointless exercise considering the station was dry—he finally began inserting pipes into the ground receptacles, then towed a heavy hose, connecting the tanker and the tanks.

The driver was short and broad-shouldered, with a wide, red-bearded ruddy face, and arms covered with tats. Inked flames shot up his neck—I hoped not indicating a death wish, given his profession. A snakeskin design that completely covered one exposed upper arm made room for an eagle and the words "Aryan Brotherhood, Florence Arizona." Strapped to his hip was a holster holding a blue carbon steel revolver. Perfectly legal in Arizona, unless he was a felon—and we had legislators who would fight for that right as well. He eyed the Latinos and they stared back at him. The connecting of pipes continued, followed by some work with dials and levers, and the driver walked back to the end of the tanker. He pulled out a red hardpack of Marlboros and lit up.

Safety first.

After taking a deep drag, he let the smoke drift out into the sunlight as he kept the cigarette hanging from his lips, folded his massive arms, and stared at the Latino kids. The revolver sat heavily on his belt.

Until then, the lane on the other side of the pumps had been empty. Now a sparkling black Cadillac SUV drove in, facing me. It had hubcaps like scimitars. They kept revolving after the vehicle came to a stop. Doors opened and five young black men stepped out into the heat. Unlike the Hispanics in their jeans and wife-beaters, they were dressed in the long-short pants that make a man look like a giant infant. None of them looked like a baby.

The closest one was taller than me and as wide as a mature tree back east, with skin the color of almonds. He ran his credit card, tugged on the gas hose, stuck it into the tank, and nothing happened. He called over to the tanker driver. The white man took another drag and showed him the finger. The black guy returned what must have been a gang sign and the Hispanics noticed.

A raised concrete island maybe three feet wide and the gas pumps separated the two groups.

Now the representing began: rival gang signs, elaborate walks toward each other only to be halted momentarily, profanities in English and Spanish. Along with this, I counted four guys raising their shirts to show firearms. Hip-hop was cranked up to compete with *banda*. More black guys appeared from another car that had parked behind the SUV: two, no, another three. All were waiting with desperate empty gas tanks, already jumpy, no doubt psychopathic, and full of tribal grudges, but they might move on if they could just fill up. They hadn't noticed me sitting there in a sedan that screamed "Unmarked Police" with my deputy's star on my belt, along with the Colt Python and one Speedloader with six extra rounds. Gasoline smells penetrated the cab of the car and a fresh sheet of sweat covered me. The Aryan tanker driver looked on impassively, finished his cigarette, and tossed it away from the vicinity of the flowing petroleum.

It was going to be a bad day all day.

I looked back at the mom, who was chatting on her cell phone, not seeming to notice the menace a few feet away. The little girl appeared more knowing, staring at the lethal theater ahead of her. I could call for backup, but people would be dead by the time the first police unit arrived. I could step out and show my badge, be the "peace officer" that Peralta once taught me, but there was no peace, not in this part of the city, not at this moment. At this moment, I should have been plotting what Peralta called a "tactical solution": which asshole I would take down first, hard enough to get the attention of the others; which assholes I would shoot, in order of their likely capabilities, if things turned to gunplay.

But, I realized, I had more assholes than I had bullets.

Peralta has said I'm good in a crisis, for an egghead. Yet my lungs throbbed with fear. The reason was simple: outside of this wide intersection of hell, I had never had more to live for.

If representing turned to violence, I had no good options, only one risky hope. One hope—for me and the little girl and everybody who would go up in the conflagration that would result that hot day. I wondered for a nanosecond if the young cops even knew the term any longer. I unhooked my badge and slipped off the holster. I untucked my dress shirt, rose up in the seat, and slipped the Python uncomfortably into my slacks behind my back. If representing turned to violence, there was only one response:

South Phoenix Rules.

I filled my lungs, reached for the car door, and started to open it when the tanker driver ambled over, unhooked his hose, and miraculously the gas pumps started to work.

Part One: The Sweet Season

Chapter One

I drove home in the light rain, watching the moisture slowly dissolve the dust that had accumulated on the windshield, then be swept aside by the wipers. The trunk of Lindsey's aging Honda Prelude was full of boxes, and the car rode low in the back. It was late December and cold for Phoenix, in the low fifties, the sky was overcast, and I wore my best suit. Up Third Avenue, the car slipped into the Willo district with its historic houses, big trees, and cooling lawns. Nearly every street had For Sale signs, a vain effort in the real-estate crash. "Willo Block Watch 9-1-1" signs had also recently proliferated in the yards, which irritated me, playing into the suburban stereotype of these neighborhoods. The really lurid crimes all happened out in the newer subdivisions.

I stopped behind a school bus letting out two children who walked east into the block of century-old bungalows on Holly Street. No children live on my block of Cypress Street. When I was their age, the neighborhood was full of kids, but it didn't have a name then. It was just a neighborhood of old houses and we all walked or rode our bikes to Kenilworth School, half a mile away. Rich kids from Palmcroft, poor kids from south of Roosevelt and the rest of us—we all went to the public school. We did duck-and-cover drills and made lifelong friends. Now the children in the neighborhood go to private schools and Kenilworth is all Hispanic and poor.

Turning onto Cypress, I saw the FedEx truck pull away from our house, the 1924 Spanish colonial with the big picture window. The tamale women were working their way toward me. It was the last week of December but I was grateful they were still peddling the homemade Christmas treat. I parked the Honda in the carport, let the boxes in the back be, and waited on the front porch. As usual, the younger woman with the good English approached courteously; the older one, perhaps the chef, stood back. I greeted them both in Spanish and held out fifteen dollars for a plastic bag of tamales. Now I had dinner.

The low sun was cutting through the clouds, hitting the Viad Tower on Central, two blocks away, just right to make it glow. It was the most interesting skyscraper in Phoenix's otherwise drab modern skyline. It was in foreclosure. On the doorstep was a square box addressed to Robin. I took the tamales in first, left them on the kitchen counter, and returned for the parcel. It was heavy. I hefted it up the staircase, past the floor-to-ceiling bookshelves, and placed it on the landing that led to the garage apartment. The apartment had its own entrance from the alley, admittedly on creaky old stairs. But Robin always came in the front door and used the open walkway that led from the land-ing, across the interior courtyard, to the south entrance of the two-room pad.

I didn't want Robin living there, even if she was Lindsey's sister. I didn't trust Robin. But Lindsey insisted that she stay; they had been separated for many years before she showed up in Phoenix outside a murder scene one afternoon. Lindsey's stubbornness about this only increased when Robin lost her job. She was a curator for a private art collection owned by one of the most prominent real-estate financiers in the city. The market collapse took down all his risky bets, and he put a nine-millimeter in his mouth. His art collection was seized. The empty shells of the projects he had funded were all over town.

Downstairs I went into our bedroom and slid off the heavy .357 in its holster, placing it in the drawer of the bedside table. Just two months ago I had been pricing gun safes. The drawer would do. I allowed myself a moment's smile: all the years Peralta had teased me about my attachment to what he called "my cannon" in an era where all the deputies carried Glocks. But it was only a moment. I kept the suit on, stared at myself in the mirror too long. Then I went into the kitchen and made a martini. Beefeater gin from the freezer, a splash of Noilly Prat vermouth, olives, stirred—the way Lindsey likes it. I settled into grandfather's leather chair in the office, tempted to read. On the top of my pile was David Kennedy's *Freedom from Fear* about the Depression years. I left it there. I thought about turning on music. I didn't. Instead I just stared into the house, stared out the picture window, and sipped the liquor. The window usually showed off our Christmas tree. This year we didn't have one.

It was an hour and a second drink later when the front door lock clicked and Robin stepped in.

"Why are you sitting in the dark, Dave?"

I told her hello, told her that she had a package. I didn't like it when she called me "Dave." That was reserved for Lindsey. Robin knew this and sensed my irritation. She shrugged and smiled. She was wearing jeans and a light leather jacket with the shoulders wet from the rain. Her hair shone in the minimal light. She was blond and tan to Lindsey's brunette and fair. Her hair was thick and unruly and it bounced against her shoulders as she walked. Lindsey's hair, nearly black it was so dark, was fine and straight as a pin. They only looked like sisters when they smiled. They shared the same watchful, ironic eyes, blue for Lindsey, gray for Robin. Pretty legs ran in the family.

"Did you hear from Lindsey Faith?"

I let my answer hang in the dark room. "No. There's tamales in the kitchen if you want some."

"Don't worry, Dave." She rushed up the stairs, disappearing from my view. "Wow, it's heavy," she said. "Maybe it's from Jax." The upstairs door opened and closed, then I heard her energetic footfall crossing above.

Yes, Jax. Her boyfriend. Jax, I liked. He was Hispanic but pronounced his name with a hard "J." I had never heard the name before, but we all have our lacunae—even washed-out history professors like me. Jax Delgado. He had aristocratic features, chiseled chin, and was well matched in the gym-rat physique for Robin. His eyes were full of life and fun—he was one of the few people I had met whose eyes fit that description of "twinkling." He had a Ph.D. in sociology from Harvard and now held tenure at NYU. Professor of American Studies, Department of Social and Cultural Analysis, his card read. It was enough to rev up my academic insecurities, except that he wore the credentials well, like a working-class kid who had made his own way but not forgotten his roots. I had enjoyed our few conversations.

He was staying in Phoenix to study sustainability. "That'll be a short paper," I had said when he told me this. "We're not sustainable." His eyes had twinkled and he said, "We'll definitely talk. You're one of the few natives I've run into."

I was looking forward to it. You had to rope in and keep the smart people in your life in Phoenix. And he seemed to calm and distract Robin, both of which were needed at this point of everybody's lives.

Now I was toasty. I should have stopped at one martini. Three tamales on a paper plate made dinner, then I grabbed Kennedy's book and went into the bedroom, closing the door. It was only a little past eight, but I felt exhausted, just like every day lately. Yet I knew I wouldn't sleep. The bed hadn't been made in days. I stretched out in it after carefully hanging up the suit. It wasn't fitting quite right. I was losing weight. Maybe if Jax had sent Robin a gift he wouldn't be joining her tonight.

For that, I'd be grateful.

That was the only rub about Jax and Robin. They were very loud when they made love. It had put an end to my winter ritual of sleeping with the windows and the screen doors to the inner courtyard open. Robin was a screamer. My first wife Patty had been one, too. We could never stay in a bed-and-breakfast. Men treasure this attribute, especially when it is genuine, and Robin sounded very genuine, and I didn't want to hear. Some people you can't imagine having sex—Peralta is one. Some you don't want to imagine having it—Robin fit there. So tonight might be quiet.

I opened the book and began to read, cradling it in one hand, letting my other arm stretch across to Lindsey's side of the bed. Herbert Hoover got a bad rap from the history mostly written by hagiographers of FDR. That was true enough. I could have written a book like this. The era was my focus in graduate school. But I didn't write this one. Hoover the great engineer, the progressive, the pain-in-the-ass as Calvin Coolidge's Commerce Secretary. He was elected president and the house fell in. Just like life. Then he was overwhelmed by events, by his own inability to think into the future, and then by his increasing isolation, intellectually and from the people…

…I felt so isolated sitting in the car at McDowell and Central, stopped at a red light. I needed to pick up Lindsey but I didn't know where she was. Light rail was gone. Central was just a wide highway again, choked with traffic. I looked northwest into Willo and it was gone, clear-cut, covered by gravel. Even the coppery Viad Tower was gone. The only sign of habitation was a new, four-story condo complex that looked as if it had been built by scavengers from a junkyard. Somehow all this seemed totally normal but it still made me feel sad. All those historic houses just gone, including mine. I wished the light would change so I didn't have to look at the emptiness.

Robin's scream woke me.

It was not a sexy scream. It was sharp, primal, terror-ridden. High voltage shot up my spine. I yanked open the bedside table drawer, grabbed the Colt Python, and rushed out the door and into the dark living room. She screamed again, called for help. I ran up the stairs with both hands on the grips of the pistol, arms crooked, barrel in the air. When the door swung open I almost brought the barrel down and shot her.

She slammed the door and smashed her body into mine. She was shivering uncontrollably. As we stood on the interior landing, I held her tightly with my left arm, keeping the gun ready and staring at the door. I tried to push her away.

"No, no, don't go back there. Please, no, don't go…"

She said this as a cascade of hysteric words strung together, as I tried to disentangle myself from her and go to the garage apartment.

"No, don't!"

I pushed her back on the landing and got as far as my hand on the doorknob.

"No! Please, David! Don't go back there!"

She decisively locked the door, flew back into my arms crying, and I held her tightly until she calmed down.

Robin is slightly taller than Lindsey. We were both completely naked.

Chapter Two

We were dressed and the revolver was back in the bedside table drawer by the time the first cops arrived, one a compact young Latino and the other an Anglo woman with her yellow hair in a bun. They regularly worked the beat in the neighborhood. I felt as if I'd been on ten thousand crime scenes, far more than the college classrooms I had taught in, a map of the twin forks my life has taken that I didn't want to think about too much that winter. Too many crime scenes, and this one happened to be at my house, the house I was raised in. And I was just one of the "subjects," as the police would say, at best a "complainant."

They strode up the staircase two steps at a time with their Glocks drawn. More cops than you realized accidentally shot themselves with their Glocks. It lacks an external safety. The internal safeties, meant to keep the semi-automatic from discharging if it's dropped, can be disengaged by a slight or accidental pull of the trigger. These two managed fine. They left the door open and crossed to the garage apartment, ordering me to remain in the living room. That was as it should be, but I wasn't used to being on the other side of the yellow tape. For years now, my deputy's badge had been the best backstage pass in town.

I already knew enough. Robin had responded to my initial questions before the first units got there, so I knew the basic information. Now she sat sullenly on the sofa next to me, having regained some of her toughness. But her eyes were still wide and she sniffled every few minutes. Robin was not a crier, much less a "hysterical female," as the dispatchers might have termed her if I had allowed her to make the 911 call. She was wearing a pair of Lindsey's sweat pants and one of Lindsey's T-shirts. I didn't like that. Now I had more questions for her, somewhere shy of a hundred, but I didn't ask. My hands shook slightly and I felt gin and tamales at the back of my throat. I realized I was in a little shock, too.

My cell was still in my hand and I had scrolled to a familiar number. Robin shook her head.

"Don't bother Lindsey Faith," she said. "It's midnight in D.C."

I put the phone away.

The Anglo cop strode back through the living room, her black shoes squeaking on the hardwood floor, and then outside. In a few minutes she was wrapping the yard with crime-scene tape. To me, it was an overreaction, but the policing business had changed since I had been a young uniformed deputy. Through the picture window, I saw a few neighbors standing on the sidewalk. It's not as if they had never seen law enforcement vehicles at our house, with both Lindsey and me working for the Sheriff's Office. A couple of years ago, a new neighbor asked around if we were having marital fights, she had seen so many cop cars stop by. We had laughed at the time. But the three hundred block of Cypress hadn't seen this. I counted the people I knew, lingered over some that I didn't. Three couples, one woman alone. Unlike most of Phoenix, Willo was a real neighborhood with plenty of walkers and it was still fairly early, not even ten o'clock.

Then we were getting the initial interview for the incident report. The female officer wrote in a tight hand. Robin did most of the talking. But this was just preliminary: names, addresses, the basic scenario—before the homicide detectives showed up.

They weren't long in arriving. My stomach gave a distinct kick when the first one walked through the door.

"Mapstone. God, I live for the day when I show up and you're in handcuffs. It might happen tonight."

"Happy New Year, Kate." I said it with just enough snark that it hit her but didn't damage any innocent bystanders.

Phoenix Police Detective Sgt. Kate Vare glared at us, hands on her hips. Underneath a PPD windbreaker, she was still compact, pinched, venomous. We had a history.

"Did you get kicked off the cold-case unit?" I smiled.

"No such luck, Mapstone. Budget cuts mean everybody's having to do more. So I have the pleasure of coming to your pile of rocks in the ghetto tonight." She ran a hand through her hair, which she had fried into a red color not found in nature. She was enjoying being taller than me for a change. "You just sit there."

"I want to go have a look."

"No way, sir," she said. "You're involved in this." She smiled widely. I had never seen Kate Vare smile before. "Anyway, you're not even a deputy any more."

I let out a long breath.

"News travels fast around the cop shop," she said, and mounted the stairs.

After she was gone, her partner, a big young guy who might have been nicknamed Moose by my parents' generation, gave me a sympathetic look. His badge was hung around his neck—one of the new ones, made to imitate the LAPD shields. It had a number in the 9000s. It made me feel old: I remembered when PPD badges were numbered in the 4000s.

He cocked his head. "It's okay." I followed him up the stairs.

Outside the wind was waving the tree branches and the overcast sky had been turned into a washed-out pink by the reflected city lights. A few stray raindrops hit my forehead. The air was cool and clean, blowing down from the High Country. Fifteen feet away, the door to the garage apartment was open and all the lights were on. One of the abstract paintings Robin had hung on the wall faced me. It was a pink moon against a green sky. She had bought it at one of the galleries on Roosevelt Row.

"Whoa, whoa, whoa, no fucking way!"

Vare charged out of the room, squared her small shoulders, and blocked us halfway. She jabbed a finger into my solar plexus. Technically, I had just been assaulted.

"This is a crime scene, you bastard. I told you to wait downstairs!"

"C'mon, Kate." Moose spoke gently. "Professional courtesy."

After a long pause, she closed the short distance between us. "If you touch anything, I swear to God…"

"I'll be good," I said. "I watch *Cops* on television all the time."

"You're not a deputy any longer, get it?"

Oh, I got it. I had turned in my badge to Peralta that morning, signed a sheaf of papers on his desk, given him my star and identification card, then spent the afternoon cleaning out my office in the old county courthouse, the room one floor below the old jail, the one that sat at the end of the corridor restored to its 1929 grandeur, with the nameplate that read David Mapstone, Sheriff's Office Historian. I would miss that room. The boxes in the Prelude held some of my work. It reminded me of the car of boxes I drove from San Diego, six years before, when I lost my teaching job and returned to Phoenix. This time I also crammed in my old metal report clipboard, my battered black Maglite, and a side-handle police baton I hadn't used in a couple of decades.

It was time to leave. I didn't want to wait until the new sheriff was sworn in. "The new sheriff." Just the words made my mouth sour up. But it was true. Peralta had been defeated in the Republican primary. I had always thought Mike Peralta would be Maricopa County Sheriff for as long as he wanted, and then become governor if he chose. But that's why historians still have jobs. When you're living events, it's hard to get perspective. And the changes that had been creeping into Phoenix for years came crashing down on my friend. Changes I had noticed, but not fully appreciated. Peralta's loss had only been one in an autumn of sorrows.

"Don't touch anything," Vare lectured.

On reflection, I think the only reason she let me go in was the hope that she could find some reason to jam me. But she turned and I followed.

Robin had decorated the large space with paintings, contemporary furniture, and a bookcase overflowing with art books.

But in my mind it was still grandmother's musty sewing room. I crept behind the cops, who were gathered around a desk that sat against the east windows. The box from the front doorstep was on the desk with its flaps open. Vare and her partner had their latex gloves on and carefully examined what was inside. It was only one thing.

From the vault of cardboard, the once-handsome features of Jax Delgado faced us like the display in a macabre shadow box. Blood was smeared across his chin. His eyes were wide open.

Chapter Three

We had no time to contemplate what had happened. More cops came, crime-lab technicians joined them, our statements were taken, the garage apartment was sealed off. It was four in the morning before we were alone again. I had a brief conversation with Lindsey, who was getting ready for work. She wanted to talk to Robin. When Robin handed the cell back to me, Lindsey said, "She's staying in the guest bedroom. Please don't argue with me about this. I'm tired." So I didn't. Her voice had sounded so unfamiliar.

The banging on the front door began at five minutes after seven. I had just come back from Starbucks with a latte for Robin and a mocha for myself. The caffeine did little for my headache and the toxic dump I felt in my stomach. Some would call it a hangover. Kate Vare stood on the front step with the rigidness of the indefatigable. She had changed into a black pants suit and had her nine in a holster on her hip.

"Come with me."

Robin looked at me apprehensively. I shrugged. Outside it was sunny and pleasant, the air dry and cleansed by last night's rain. I saw the blue-and-white Phoenix Police cruiser parked in the driveway.

"Leave those drinks," Vare commanded.

"Fuck you, Kate." I was exhausted and cross even before this petite gift of hell had shown up on my doorstep for the second time in less than twelve hours. "Arrest me if you don't like it. Come on, Robin."

Vare stomped ahead and opened a back door.

"The brass take away your ride?"

"Get in."

I knew her game. Make us ride in the prisoner compartment. Make us nervous. Oh, and repay me for all the alleged slights over the years when my work on cold cases had somehow crossed the red line of her jurisdiction and her ego.

"Watch your head." She put her hand on top of Robin's head as she scrunched down and slid onto the seat, just like it happens with real prisoners.

"Watch your head, sir." It didn't work quite the same with me. I was too tall for her to guide me down, so she didn't try.

"Thank you for your concern, officer."

She ignored me and slammed the door. It lacked any visible locks, of course. We were essentially prisoners. The backs of patrol cars had changed since I was a young deputy, on my first sojourn into law enforcement before going back to graduate school. In those days, the older cars lacked any protection; suspects just sat in the back seat. The newer ones had rudimentary cage wire to protect the officers sitting in front. Now the prisoner compartment was much more elaborate, and confining, with Plexiglas ahead of us and heavy bars protecting the side windows, to keep suspects from kicking out the glass, wiggling out, and running away. I had seen it happen. Now I just sipped my mocha as Vare drove fast down Fifth Avenue to the Papago Freeway.

"Are you taking us straight to the tent jail?" I spoke through the Plexiglas. She wasn't driving toward downtown.

"God, how I wish." And that was all she said.

She drove west, took the 35th Avenue exit, and turned toward the South Mountains until she reached Lower Buckeye Road. A collection of ramshackle houses, tilt-up warehouses, and junkyards provided the scenery. The big county complex was off to one side. I avoided looking that way. The inside of the car smelled; it was better for my stomach not to attempt to pick out the origins of the odors. Robin made the mistake of touching the thick vinyl of the seat and withdrew her hand. Her face was tense, her mouth compressed into a thin line barely holding in emotions. Her coffee sat undrunk, her free hand balled up in a fist.

She had thought she was getting a gift from her lover and had waited to open it until after dinner. She hoped he would be joining her as a surprise. She undressed, lit a candle, and poured a glass of wine in anticipation. The X-Acto knife cut easily through the packing tape. Jax's head had been covered with a layer of bubble wrap that had made identification impossible until she had pulled it off—and there he was. Robin had told me this story before the cops arrived and hadn't deviated from it despite hours of Kate Vare's badgering. I didn't trust Robin for my own reasons, but she had nothing to do with this crime.

At 51st Avenue, a large field was still left on the southwest corner. I couldn't identify the crop—maybe alfalfa?—but the view was a time machine into old Phoenix, the place where I had grown up. If you blocked out an ugly brown subdivision a couple of miles south, the vista was magnificent. Green field running toward the rough, treeless mountains in the distance under a vault of pure Western sky. It gave me a moment's solace. I just watched the land and felt my chest fill with breath. Then Vare jerked the car to the right and we were inside a housing development.

One way in and out, surrounded by an outside wall, curvy streets, look-alike stucco houses with large driveways, big garages, and small front doors. No shade. It was unremarkable for what passed for a "neighborhood" in most of Phoenix, except that it looked mostly unoccupied, with a trail of For Sale signs along the street Vare drove. I saw two PPD units sitting in the asphalt gulf where the street curved north. It held three houses closely sandwiched into the bend. The door to one tan house was standing open, guarded by a uniform.

Vare turned in the seat. "Does your friend recognize this house, Mapstone?"

"She's got a name and she can speak for herself. Unless you're arresting us and then we're not saying a damned thing…"

Robin interrupted. "I've never been here in my life." She took a long draw on the latte and ran her other hand through her tousled hair, pulling it back over her shoulder, trying to tuck part of the strands under her ears. She watched me watch her as the car door opened.

Vare led us beneath the festive yellow tape and into the house. At the entryway, we all put on light blue crime-scene booties. I didn't like the smell. But we followed her through the narrow entry hall and back into the sunny, high-ceilinged Arizona room. There was no furniture, no drapes. She pointed into the kitchen, where a body was slung over the top of the center island. It was the body of a man, completely naked. Blood had dripped down the counter tiles onto the new floor. It was mostly dry. Robin gave a small animal's alarm call, covered her mouth, and ran back outside.

"Crime scene's on the way. Don't touch anything." Vare laid her hand on the butt of her Glock.

"Don't accidentally shoot yourself, Kate," I said. I breathed through my mouth, which would help for a while, before I started to taste the rotting odor. Thank God it wasn't in summer. The body hadn't been here long—long enough for rigor to go away, twelve hours give-or-take as I recalled—but not long enough to putrefy and swell. I kept my distance, walking slowly in an orbit of six feet away. It wasn't that I hadn't seen bodies. I just didn't want the tightly wound living body in the black pants suit to freak out and make me leave.

The dead body belonged to a male about my height with an athletic build. His thighs, calves, and hands were bloody from wounds. One hand was larger than the other. A large pool of blood congealed between his legs, which were slightly open. I stepped around a cordless drill. It had a small, bloody bit in its mouth. Close to the refrigerator, a stained handsaw lay on the fashionable Spanish tiles of the upgraded kitchen. The body was missing its head.

Even in Phoenix, there probably weren't that many headless bodies at the moment.

"Jax." I whispered it.

Vare shook her head. "Is that his name? Your girlfriend's…"

"She's…not!" Something in my voice actually made her take a step back.

"Well, she's looking at some major trouble, Mapstone. She's lying. I can tell it. You can, too—don't deny it. I can't tell if you're lying because I never believe you anyway. You both had better start cooperating."

I asked her how she had found the body. It didn't look as if any of the neighboring houses were occupied, so this was no place for a block watch. A tip, she said.

"A tip? From where? What kind of tip?" I turned away from the corpse and faced her straight on, trying not to let my anger take over. It wasn't easy.

"I can't tell you that, sir," she said, wagging a finger at me, emphasizing that last word, leaving no doubt that I was now just a *civilian*. She had a large gold wedding band on her hand with diamonds in it. Somebody once told me she had three children. I couldn't imagine. She went on, "Let's go through it again. Jax Delgado…"

So I went through it again: I'd known him for six weeks, since about the time he and Robin had started dating. She met him at a First Friday gallery exhibit. Lindsey and I liked him and invited them both for drinks and dinner. His grandfather was from Cuba and he'd grown up in Miami. I'd seen him maybe a dozen times, mostly fleeting.

"You'd better notify New York University," I said. "He's on the faculty. They'll have next-of-kin information."

Vare laughed, showing her prominent incisors. "Mapstone, if you're telling the truth, you're a fucking idiot."

"It wouldn't be the first time both those things were true."

The new voice was deep, commanding, familiar. I turned my head to see Mike Peralta filling my vision. Behind him was Robin.

Vare rounded on him. "This is not your jurisdiction. You're almost ou…" She stopped herself.

Peralta smiled slightly. "Everything is my jurisdiction, Kate. For a few more days, at least."

Chapter Four

The uniformed cops in the entry hall had already made room for the big man in the tan suit. His thick hair was combed straight back from a wide forehead and the years had turned it from black to charcoal. His face: carve it into a mountainside. You had to know how to watch his eyes and mouth to see what was really going on inside him. Now he walked into the room with his deliberate tread. His dark eyes ignored mine, taking in the scene even as his head barely moved. Robin stood beside him, her hand on his arm. Two of her could have fit inside him.

"Is this him?" Peralta spoke with uncommon gentleness. Robin nodded.

"What's that, Miss Bryson? I need a positive identification." Kate Vare took Robin by the arm and led her close to the body, waving an outstretched arm as if she were showing off a new car. "Was this the man you had been seeing?"

Robin wrapped her arms tightly across her sweatshirt, pushing up her breasts. Vare kept hold of her. "Yes." Her eyes were wide and wet. "It's Jax."

"How do you know?"

"We were lovers." Robin's skin grew pale.

"Accomplices, maybe?" Vare held her close to the corpse.

Robin shook her head adamantly. "You don't know anything."

Vare released her grip. "Now I want these civilians outside."

Peralta held up a hand. "Robin can sit in my car. Mapstone is still a deputy sheriff."

Vare's face dropped in dismay.

"I haven't put through his papers yet." He reached in his suit-coat pocket, produced my sheriff's office identification card, then pinned it onto my shirt like a shabby medal. Peralta said, "I think we'll both see what you've got."

"Well, Mapstone's history won't do any good here," Vare sulked. Peralta might have been the outgoing sheriff, but he was still close friends with the police chief, so she was stuck with us.

"La Fam?"

"Looks that way," Vare answered.

Peralta grunted. I stood back, trying to keep up.

He produced a set of latex gloves and snapped them on, then stood over the kitchen island like a surgeon examining the work of a demented colleague.

"So did you track the package?" He already knew what had happened. It had only been twenty-four hours since I had last seen him, but somehow it seemed longer. I couldn't tell whether I was glad to see him here or not. Considering Kate Vare was the lead investigator, I decided I was delighted.

Vare spoke reluctantly, pausing to give me the cop eye. "It was sent from the FedEx Office store on Central, uptown, you know, the old Kinko's. Fake name and address of the sender. We're going to interview the employee who saw the sender later this morning."

Peralta nodded and went back to the corpse.

I heard one young uniform whisper to another: "Jax in the Box. May I take your order?" Another: "It gives a whole new meaning to giving head."

Peralta's voice overrode them. "They tortured him with the drill…" He pointed to the dark craters on his legs and the top of one hand, then he stepped lightly in a counter-clockwise circle, his eyes scanning, his head momentarily shielded by his back and broad shoulders. "Slit open his scrotum. That was probably late in the game."

He turned back to the rest of us and pointed. "See his left hand? That's from being dipped in boiling water repeatedly. Make sure crime scene gets that shot."

Vare just had to stand there and take it. Her tight frame was almost humming with tension. I wondered if the black pants suit would burst into flames. I loved it. She said, "Yes, Sheriff."

Emerson said there is no history, only biography. If that's true, Mike Peralta encapsulated much of what was worth knowing about the best of law enforcement in Phoenix, not to mention more of my life than I cared to dwell on at that moment. I'd first met him when he was a trainer at the academy, then he had broken me in as my first partner.

We remained friends for the years I lived away from Phoenix, teaching in Ohio and San Diego. He never stopped saying that it was a mistake for me to be anything but a cop, and when I came home after my first marriage broke up he gave me a job. A pile of old cases—clean them up, he said. So I did, using the historian's techniques married to my cop knowledge. It became a full-time job, working the crimes that ran from the 1960s all the way back to statehood. I didn't fool myself: It had been good publicity for the sheriff to have an egghead on staff. I also solved some major cases. The old ID card hung familiarly from my pocket.

"La Fam," I said. "I didn't think they had a big presence here."

I heard the naiveté in my voice even before I finished the sentence. La Familia was one of the most notorious gangs in Mexico and Southern California. Its signature execution was beheading. I cleared my throat. "But it wouldn't be surprising to see them expanding with all the destabilization caused by the recession."

Peralta's eyes fixed on me. They said, shut up. I looked down at the blood spatter on the floor. Gangs were nothing new to Phoenix. Contrary to the local feel-good spin, Phoenix had been a Mafia hangout for decades. Some old cops told me that it had more mobsters per capita than New York City in the 1950s. It was close to the mob's operations in Vegas, close to the border, easy to be anonymous. They hung out at places like the Blue Grotto, the Clown's Den, Durant's, Rocky's Hideaway, and the Ivanhoe. Old Phoenix had been a paradise with snakes, indeed. It's what kept my nostalgia for what had been lost from slipping

into the lie of sentimentality. But I admitted to myself that I
was way behind on the gangs of today, aside from knowing they
were large, sophisticated, and deadly. That knowledge rarely penetrated my office in the old courthouse, where the crimes were as
old as the architecture around me and where Peralta deliberately
kept me segregated from the rest of the Sheriff's Office.

"Did you know this subject, Sheriff?" Vare asked, tilting her
sharp chin toward the corpse.

"I met him once. Seemed nice enough." Peralta slid off the
gloves and handed them to one of the young cops. There'd
been a time, when the Arizona Dreams case was busted open,
when I thought Peralta and Robin might actually become an
item. It had never happened and I didn't know why. That was
fine with both Lindsey and me. It would have led to too many
complications. And we still missed Peralta's ex-wife Sharon. Mike
as chief deputy and then sheriff, Sharon as a psychologist and
best-selling author: They were a power couple without airs. It
seemed impossible to imagine him with anyone else. Knowing
him, I suspected he didn't want anyone trying to get close now.
The cops, that was what he was all about, and now even that was
gone. Of course, he didn't lack for job offers, all of them paying
more than the post of Maricopa County Sheriff. I wondered for
a few seconds where he might end up. It helped shave the edge
off my emotions.

Peralta stepped back and thrust his hands into his pockets,
pushing back his wide-cut suit coat enough so that I could
see the .45 in his shoulder rig. He faced Vare. "So why would
Professor Delgado here have ended up with La Fam? Unless he
wasn't who he claimed to be…"

"That's the whole deal!" Vare's voice trembled in agitation. I
felt my chest grow tight. "He's a fraud. There's no Jax Delgado
on the NYU faculty, contrary to what Mapstone and the girl
keep telling me." She glared at me. "Oh, you're surprised?"

"How…?" It was all I could manage.

"He's not on the faculty. Nobody by that name. Nobody
matching his description. We emailed a photo. No, Mapstone,

we didn't wait. We woke people up. This is a major case. Somebody beheaded by La Familia in Phoenix, or a La Fam copycat—whatever—and the head shipped to a woman who lives in a historic district? If the media get hold of this it won't be just another forgotten asshole-on-asshole homicide in Scaryvale."

"What about this cat's ID?"

"No wallet, nothing on the body. No clothes left." She leaned toward him. "Sheriff, I hate to tell you, but the girl is lying and I wonder about Mapstone here."

"We all do, Kate. But I'm going to give them a ride home now. You got your positive ID. You know where to find Mapstone and Robin."

"What's that under the drill?" I said.

I had been desperately searching for gravity as they were talking and my eyes had wandered. Something the color of dull silver was sitting beneath handle of the power drill.

Vare just stood there, as if anything I said was illegitimate, but Peralta took out a cheap plastic pen and slightly lifted the tool from the floor. I was expecting to see a bolt and learn some new, unwanted information about torture, but no. Underneath was a ring. Vare knelt—her knees cracked—and lifted it in her gloved hand. Peralta gently let the drill down exactly where it had sat.

"Shit." She said it quietly. Then she held it up for the sheriff to see.

He bent towards her, squinting. "It might be a copycat," he said. "A wanna-be."

"Maybe," she said, unconvinced. "It looks like platinum. Not cheap."

I moved over to them, bent down on my haunches. It was a man's signet ring with a sharp engraving protruding from it.

It was an image of a rattlesnake's head.

I said, "Kate, it's you."

"Asshole," she said quietly.

"El Verdugo." Peralta spoke with gravity and fluency. My Spanish was rusty but I knew the word. "The executioner." Nobody said anything for at least a minute.

I held out my hands, waiting.

Vare sounded like my fourth-grade teacher lecturing the bad kids in the front row. "Pedro Alejandro Vega. Big-time hit man for the Sinaloa cartel. When he kills, he leaves the ring's implant on the victim's forehead. Like an artist signing a painting."

"I've never seen Jax wear that ring."

"That doesn't mean shit," Vare said. "There's no photo of Vega. He's never been arrested. He's almost like a folklore legend in the narcocorridos." She rolled her r's, something I could never master, using the word for the songs that romanticized the exploits of the drug world. "Your Jax could easily be Pedro Vega. And then, I've got a whole list of new questions for you and this Robin Bryson."

"Whatever." Anger burned my throat. I processed, trying to see the world as it was, not as I wanted it to be. The foulness of the air was now in my taste buds.

"If La Fam killed El Verdugo..." Vare was talking to herself, tucking her head down, saying words that would confuse any Iowans who just moved to town but were obviously of great interest to the PPD. She dropped the ring into a plastic evidence envelope, muttered profanities. "What the hell was he doing in Phoenix, posing as a college professor?"

"That's not my problem, Kate," I said. "Sounds like a gang-unit deal, and you can go back to trying to close screwed-up cases from the eighties."

Chapter Five

I stalked out into the sunlight where Robin was leaning against the hood of Peralta's black Crown Victoria, her sunglasses on, staring down a street of bank-owned houses that was empty except for the police cars. A crime-scene van was pulling up. The two plainclothes deputies in Peralta's security detail sat in another Crown Vic. They waved. I nodded. I felt like a chump. It was okay. It was a good feeling, in fact, like the clean air I was sucking in to get the smell of dead body to leave my head.

Sure, I'd had a couple of good cocktail conversations with Jax Delgado about Churchill as a wartime leader and our current endless wars, and about the civilizations of Mesoamerica. But anybody can read a book. Anybody can play a role. He could be a cartel killer from Sinaloa. I'd been played, made a chump. I laughed inside and shook my head. Considering the weights around my heart the past few months, being played was almost a holiday.

But this amusement was a product of one hour's sleep in the past forty-eight hours. It was a feeling, a wish. It wasn't a thought. My eyes found Robin, surprised by how uncharacteristically fragile she appeared. Then Vare caught up with me.

"I'll be in touch, smartass," she said. "In the meantime, you'd better be wondering why the severed head of El Verdugo was sent to your house. And you'd better get Ms. Bryson and check into a motel. Let me know where you go."

I am not generally a stupid person, but of course what she said was as obvious as a mountain falling on me. But my emotions had been living moment-to-moment lately. Combine it with the turmoil of the past four months, a bad hangover, and the suffocating feeling of being in the death house and you get a stupid person. All the weights stacked back up inside me.

"You will protect her," I said.

Vare shook her head. "I could lock her up as a material witness. I might still do it."

I told her that wasn't what I meant.

"Do you understand budget cuts, Mapstone?"

"Don't make this personal, about you and me, Kate. They know where she lives. They know she was seeing him. So they were sending her a message, like 'you're next'—and you're telling me you won't protect her?"

She moved close in, poked me in the chest with her finger. "That's exactly what I'm saying, you worthless-piece-of-shit excuse for anything. Right now she's a suspect. If she wants my help, she'd better start telling the truth. Otherwise, she's your problem, fuck-face." Spittle came out of her angry mouth, shining in the sunlight. "You're a deputy sheriff." She snapped my ID card with her nail. "I feel better about her safety already."

She spun around and stomped back into the house, nearly colliding with the supertanker of Peralta.

Now two unmarked PPD Chevies came speeding down the new pavement of the street. Two pairs of detectives got out: slim, young, male, shorthaired. They walked over to Peralta and shook his hand, telling them they were sorry he had lost the election. He nodded and clapped them on their arms.

"I'll be fine," he said. They slid under the crime-scene tape and walked to the house.

"They probably voted against you," I said.

"Nah. If the new sheriff really does what he promised and uses the department to play Border Patrol, it's going to complicate things for every agency. People in the immigrant neighborhoods will go back to fearing the police. We worked years to overcome that. Worse, more paperwork."

His normally immobile face managed a wink.

"You're pretty fucking tranquil about all this!" My hands ached from the fists they had been unconsciously molded into for who-knows-how-long. "Here, take this goddamned thing." I handed him my identification card. Robin gave me what might have been a look of concern or sympathy. I ignored her.

I felt Peralta's large arm steer me aside and move me down the sidewalk.

"You have an anger-management problem, Mapstone."

Peralta was the most cant-free person I had ever known. The world turned upside down again and it only made me madder.

"You sound like Sharon now!" I was baiting him. I didn't care. His voice was calm.

"Mapstone, you have been the moodiest son of a bitch the past few months. It was just an election. The voters have spoken, the bastards." His eyebrows subtly philosophized with each other. The corners of his mouth raised a few millimeters. "I came up with that. Pretty good, huh?"

"You didn't come up with it. Mo Udall said it."

"Whatever. I'm the one who lost the election, not you. People fall for this 'be scared of the Mexicans' crap, even though they want cheap housecleaning and lawn care and never wonder why their homes are inexpensive." He sighed. "Anyway, you'll do fine. You're going to be a professor again, right?"

I tentatively nodded. It seemed that I was in line to become an adjunct professor at ASU. The pay was crap and it lacked tenure track, but any money would help. I had other misgivings: about the tough university president, about the mega-department in which history resided, about my own inability to catch up with the latest politically correct fads. But the ASU people made it sound enticing: I could teach in a multi-disciplinary field: Phoenix history, criminal justice, courses I could put together. It would do until Lindsey and I decided our future. I loved teaching. I needed the distraction of work.

"So what's bugging you?"

"Things." I stared at the pavement. The all-too-familiar empty ache returned to my middle.

"You look like crap this morning. You didn't even shave. How's your wife?"

"She's fine."

He cocked his head. "Maybe you'll end up in Washington, Mapstone. Lindsey was one of my best. I'm glad she took the job. She could become a star at Homeland Security."

"She's trying it out for six months." I heard the anxiety in my voice.

"Sure," he said. "Is Robin telling the truth?"

I told him, yes. At least I thought so.

He put his bear-paw hand against my shoulder. It was not a friendly bear.

"Look, this is serious shit she's landed in. They know where she lives. They know where you live. Get it? Vare is right. You need to get out of the house. You guys can come up to my place, if you want. Plenty of room. I'm hardly ever home. But Robin may know more than she even realizes. She might have seen something, overheard something."

"What if she didn't?"

"Whoever tortured that man, whether he was El Verdugo or a professor, and then sent his fucking head to your house, thinks she did." His voice rose ever so slightly, his anger evident to a close observer of all-things-Peralta. The bear paw came down. "And you'd better get your shit together and focus."

We walked back to his Crown Vic. Robin had tied her hair into a ponytail. He put her in the front seat. I got in back and tried to focus.

I focused on Robin's neck, which bore a similarity to my missed love. Lindsey and Robin both had long, elegant necks. Lindsey's hair brushed against her neck and shoulders as she turned her head. It was art in sensual motion. Just thinking about it could make me feel better.

Then I saw the chain sitting against Robin's skin. I had never noticed it before. It was a simple ball chain, like the kind that hangs from a bare-bones lamp, one gray kernel snapped into the other.

This chain had blood on it.

Chapter Six

I kept my discovery to myself as Peralta drove us home. My temples throbbed.

Something was different in his manner as we turned down Cypress Street. He stopped chatting about nothing with Robin. I watched the back of his head. It swiveled just enough. He was taking the street in, checking out the houses. Not even a lawn crew was there but he drove past my house, went around the block on Holly, past the little park we used to call Paperboys' Island, and returned to Cypress. My hands grew cold. After stopping he came inside with us and casually asked Robin to run through the events of the previous night. As she did, they walked through the house. He was leading. His walk was looser and more attentive. As she talked, he was silent, just nodding. He reminded her of the offer for us to stay at his place and gave me a look that said, "back outside."

"You're checking out the house," I said once we were on the walk.

"Can't beat this weather, Mapstone." It was seventy degrees, cloudless, dry, and he was lying to me.

I pulled on his suit coat and he stopped, turning to face me.

"How did you know about this?"

His eyes widened with too much innocence. "You know the watch commander briefs me every morning on what went down the night before all over the county, especially the one-eighty-sevens." The homicides. "The address sounded familiar."

"I bet."

He strode to the car and I followed him. We both scanned the streetscape. He was just able to do it more casually, mostly moving his eyes. He slid a key into the trunk and it popped open.

"Here."

"I don't need that. It looks too small anyway."

"It's for Robin."

I hesitated, then took the Kevlar vest in one hand. "So I'm supposed to tell her about this El Verdugo? Let her know she's in a lot worse danger than the trauma of opening that FedEx carton? That her boyfriend wasn't a professor who studied at Harvard but was a killer for the Sinaloa cartel? Hell, no. You do it. And tell her she has to wear this damned thing. She might actually do what you say. She likes you."

"She likes you, too. It makes you uncomfortable."

"Oh, bullshit! You know something. You know more than you're telling me."

He ignored me. A large black bag was hefted halfway out of the trunk and I heard a heavy zipper. He held out a semi-automatic pistol.

"Is that for her, too?"

"This is for you."

Now my dread was complete. He was arming me up. I mumbled a quiet protest about the Colt Python. I was not a semi-auto man. That wasn't really where my brain was: We were on our own. Kate Vare and PPD were not going out of their way to help Robin. And all I had in the house was my .357 magnum.

I took the new pistol as if in a trance.

It was unfamiliar: a black semi-automatic, sleek grip, futuristic frame that tapered into the barrel, no visible hammer, gray polymer controls including the safety on the side. It had a small cylinder attached to the accessory rail: a laser sight. This was the business, nasty looking. And that was before I saw the ammunition. The rounds looked like small rifle cartridges, with blue on their missile-sharp tips.

"This is an FN Five-Seven, from Belgium. This can inspire you to study Belgium history."

"You don't strike me as a Walloonophile."

"Fuck you, too." He had no idea what I was talking about.

The pistol was amazingly light, half the weight of the .357. I popped the magazine and racked the slide mechanism to make sure it was empty. I studied the small bullets.

"The rounds are half the size of a nine, but they're better," he said. "This holds twenty rounds and one in the chamber. Here's another two magazines." I stuffed them in my pants pockets. Back his head and shoulders went into the trunk. He handed me a small slide-belt holster. Then a silver-plated .38 Chief's Special.

"Teach Robin about this one. It's a good gun for a girl. That's all I've got in the car that doesn't belong to the county," he went on.

"I can't believe you. I'm not a deputy now! Can't you call the chief? Get Vare to give some protection?"

He shrugged. "I can try. There are limits to friendship, especially when you're a lame-duck Mexican."

I kept the guns, my hands full of weaponry as if visited by a violent Santa, but I didn't like the semi-auto's small bullets. Stopping power was everything. Peralta had taught me that. He obsessed about it. A .22 will eventually kill a suspect, but it won't stop him if he's determined to keep coming. The Python will knock a man down and kill him instantly.

He said, "Those five-seven rounds will penetrate ballistic Kevlar vests. Don't worry. Anyway, you might need both guns and more."

He slammed the trunk lid down and prepared to get in the car.

"I can't believe you're cutting out." That didn't faze him. He sat heavily in the driver's seat. I desperately talked ammo to keep him there. "If these rounds will penetrate a vest, what if the bad guys use one on Robin?"

"Don't let that happen."

I didn't wait to watch him drive away. I went inside and stashed the gear in my bedroom. Sitting on the edge of the bed, I felt a momentary paralysis set in, starting in my feet and moving quickly to the brain. We lacked the money to move to a motel for any length of time. I didn't want to be stuck out at Peralta's big house overlooking Dreamy Draw. I needed some time away from him, his moods, and demands. This house represented almost everything of financial value we had, and a value much greater to me. Just leave it? Let them fire bomb it? I would lose the last thing my family had passed on to me. I would lose grandfather's desk, Lindsey's gardens. I would lose the library.

I closed the door. Lindsey answered on the fifth ring.

"Am I calling at a bad time?"

That stranger's voice came back at me, the one that had emerged since September, the one that kept sticking a baseball bat into my stomach every time I heard it. I loved Lindsey's voice, at one time thinking I knew every mood and desire firing it. Of course I was wrong. The personal calamity that overtook us was like an earthquake in a place with strong building codes, only the buildings didn't stand. I had always thought such an event would cause us to cleave closer, but I was wrong.

Things, indeed, fell apart, the magical golden light of fall providing no balm. My love became unreachable. The holidays were especially grim, that day between Thanksgiving and Christmas when Lindsey lay on her stomach on the bed, her right leg bent up, twitching like a metronome, and she told me she had taken a job with Homeland Security. It was an announcement, not an invitation to discussion. She would move to Washington, D.C.—alone. She couldn't be in the house. She needed time away from me. This was how much our personal disaster had shifted the axis on what I once thought was the most stable terra firma.

I tried talking about us but she cut me off.

"You always want to talk things out, Dave. Some things can't be fixed by talking."

Still. I brought her up to date and told her Robin needed to come to Washington, to stay with her. To hell with Kate Vare if she didn't like it.

"No," the stranger's voice said. "David…" A deep exhaustion shaded her intonations. "I can't deal with this right now. I just can't."

"I need your help, Lindsey."

"You're badgering me!"

"I'm not trying to…"

"Then you have to handle this. I need you to protect Robin. Do what you need to do. But she can't come here. It's impossible."

I wanted to ask why, but she was gone even before I could tell her I loved her.

In such a mood, I walked into the kitchen and found Robin standing by the window. She was staring out at the orange trees in the increasingly unkempt back yard, drinking orange juice. Any bad guy outside could shoot her that second.

"David, I'm sorry…" She set the glass down. "For all this."

I walked close to her, wavered inside for a moment, then put my hand on the arc of her cheek. She had regained her color. The skin-on-skin momentarily rattled and confused me. She leaned against my hand and smiled. Small, attractive crinkles appeared at the edges of her eyes.

I regained my mental footing and let my fingers slide down to the simple metal chain on her neck, then slip under it and pull it out onto the sweatshirt. Metal slapped on metal. She jumped back three steps.

"Sorry." She smiled. "Tickled." Her face blushed the red of the apprehended. She slid the chain back under the sweatshirt, freed her hair, and fluffed it out. I had my reasons for not trusting Robin. But I had never imagined she could be involved in a murder. Until now.

"How much did you know about Jax?" I spoke the name as if it still meant something.

"Things you know when you've been seeing a man for a couple months." She finished the orange juice and put the glass in the dishwasher.

"The cops don't think his name is Jax. They think his name is Pedro Alejandro Vega." I watched her eyes and mouth; they registered confusion. I went on and told her what I knew, he was a hit man, involved in one of the most dangerous drug cartels in the world.

She shook her head as I talked. After an hour with Peralta, it was always surprising to be with someone with an expressive face. Robin's eyes were wide and teary. She wiped her too-long nose. Her jaw worked in agitation. Little ripples of emotion shook her cheeks. She was two years younger than Lindsey, yet looked instantly older.

I stepped closer. "He told you this, didn't he?"

She stepped back again. "Of course not! Are you crazy?"

"You suspected…"

"No! He's a professor! He couldn't hurt a fly. I was afraid he was too nice a guy to hold my interest, for God's sake."

"And you had no suspicions? None?"

"None." Her hair shook vigorously.

I let her keep her distance as I spoke again. "Why is there blood on that chain?"

Robin's hand went unconsciously to her breastbone. She opened her mouth but nothing came out.

"I saw it on the back of your neck in the car. It has blood spatter on it."

"David, you don't understand." She started out past me but I stopped her. Her face went through stages, settling on surprised fury. "You son of a bitch!" She threw a punch, a good one. I caught it just in time. Grabbing her roughly by the arm, I pushed her into the breakfast nook.

"We're going to talk." I reached across and pulled the chain out again. It held two dog tags. They were bare metal, without the rubber cushions that soldiers had started using in Vietnam to keep the tags from making noise. That would make them from World War II or Korea. The metal had aged into a dark gray, although the raised information stamped into the tag was still silvery. The dog tags themselves looked clean. Indeed, the entire part of the chain I could see now was spotless. The bloodstains were only on the back, as if they had been missed during a quick cleaning.

She saw my appraisal and again covered the tags with her hand. Her face turned redder and a vein stood out in her forehead. "Why am I being questioned?" Her voice echoed around the wood of the old breakfast nook. "Jax has been killed! I lost my lover! You're just being an asshole cop, just like the rest. It's what you've become, David! Why are your losses this big deal and mine is nothing?"

"This isn't about me."

Her eyes were molten. "Yes, it is. It's been all about you, about you and Lindsey Faith! My grief is shit to you. You think I'm guilty of something."

I forced my breathing to slow down. Quietly, I asked her how the chain got bloody. Maybe it was totally innocent. She had been wearing it, this chain I had never seen on her before, yesterday when she opened the box. And maybe, just maybe, it had fallen into the blood. I didn't believe it.

"Jax gave it to me."

"He gave it to you, or you took it?"

She tried to get up. I pushed her back again. I looked at my sister-in-law anew. I couldn't tell what the hell I saw except… capacity. To lie, to conceal evidence, what else? My mouth felt as if it was stuffed with gauze. "You took this out of the FedEx box, washed it, and kept it from the police…"

After a long silence, she nodded. "I guess I did."

Now my stomach had a hole straight through it. "Was that before or after you screamed last night?"

Her eyes grew wide and wet again. "Everything happened fast, all right? But it was right there. And it mattered. So I did it. Now you can arrest me and all your fucking problems will be over, David, except they won't."

"Our problems are just beginning." I said it quietly. She had taken evidence, tampered with it. A crime. Unless I called Kate Vare that moment, I was a part of it.

The house was silent for a long time. Finally, Robin took off the chain and rested it gently on the table.

"This was the most important thing in the world to him. He told me that if anything ever happened, he wanted me to have it." She touched it tenderly, then slid it toward me. "He wanted me to show it to you. He said you'd know what it meant."

Chapter Seven

She slid the dog tags at me like Kryptonite. It made me think of the Superman comics I collected as a kid. I had filled a cardboard citrus box full of them, and today they'd really be worth money, but somewhere along the way I dumped them. I was having too many such magical thinking moments lately. Exhaustion, fear, and anger competed for my emotional center. I ran the Arizona Revised Statutes through my head, counting all the laws I was on the verge of violating. I stopped at seven.

Then I looked over at Robin again. She had shown up unexpectedly a year before, Lindsey's half-sister, a woman she barely knew as an adult. And yet she had become important to Lindsey. Vital, especially the past few months. Now my one undamaged connection to Lindsey was ensuring this woman's protection. I picked up the tags and examined them.

The information stamped into the two-inch-long, aged metal was basic: a name, serial number followed by some other numerals, another name and an address, all on five lines. There was a small notch in the end of each tag. I had wanted to study military history, but the discipline was frowned upon when I was in graduate school. My advisor had urged me to consider gender studies. But I was enough of an amateur scholar to know this data was from World War II. The numbers "43-45" indicated the years of immunization shots. The soldier's blood type was O. He was a Protestant. The name and address were whom to notify in case of emergency. They went to Poston, Arizona. And the soldier's name was Johnny Kurita. It was as far from the Sinaloa cartel, or a Hispanic academic from New York, as you could get.

"Nisei," I said.

"The second generation," Robin said. "The children of Japanese immigrants to America."

I nodded, pleasantly surprised. Outside of her art knowledge, Robin had always seemed street smart rather than book smart, certainly not well versed in my dying discipline. I said, "The Poston address makes sense, too. Lots of Nisei were forcibly interned in World War II. Poston was a camp." I hated to use the words, but they were accurate. "An American concentration camp."

"And yet this Johnny Kurita was in the service?"

"The Nisei soldiers were famous for their bravery."

"Why would they fight for a country that had done that to them?"

I let that sit. "What was Johnny Kurita to Jax?"

"He never said. But he always wore the chain and dog tags. I'd ask him about it, but he'd just say it was a memento. Something passed on to him. But it was really like an amulet to him. He'd touch it almost obsessively. When he took it off and let me hold it, I knew I was getting somewhere."

"He didn't explain it? No story behind it?"

"He said, 'when I get to know you better.' But that didn't happen." Her voice choked.

"And yet he said if anything happened to him, to give it to me..."

"Yes, that was about a week ago."

"When, exactly."

"Don't be such a bastard, David. That's not really you." She screwed up her brow. "It was last Thursday night. We'd made love. I was touching his chest and playing with the dog tags. He put his hand on mine and said it. When I asked him about it, he just smiled and said, 'it's no big deal. Just a thought.' I didn't know what he meant."

"Was he worried? Had anyone made threats against him?"

She shook her head. "There were never any threats. He was kind of a loner, which I appreciate. So I never met his friends here, if he had any. And he was new to town. He did seem distracted that night. Not quite himself."

"Maybe he had somebody to kill."

"He wasn't a hit man!"

I asked her about where they went on dates. It was nothing out of the ordinary, although from the names of some of the restaurants they patronized it was clear he had money. Did he run into any old acquaintances? Anybody who might have seen her with him, and somehow chose her to send this horrific message? No. Did she ever feel as if they were being followed when they drove back here? No.

"Did he have drugs?"

"Of course not. I hate drugs."

"Not even a little pot between friends? C'mon." Even my first wife, Patty, had a fondness for the occasional toke—and the marijuana she procured was much more potent than the stuff I tried in college. It was another life; I shelved the thought away.

Robin glared at me. Of course that information meant nothing. The high-end people in the cartels usually don't use their products. They don't want to get careless.

I stopped talking, stood, and fetched a clear plastic bag from the drawer, then dropped the dog tags inside. She gave them to me, as he had asked. I knew what they meant in a historical sense. But that did nothing to solve the murder, or answer why the man's head was delivered to my sister-in-law. That act spoke for itself: just as Peralta had said, the killers had connected her to Jax, and not in a casual way, and they knew where she lived.

In the study, I removed a sheaf of file folders from the deep desk drawer, and then replaced them on top of the bag. Concealing evidence. Add it to my rap sheet.

The phone rang. I let it go to the answering machine and heard a woman's voice. She was a news producer for Channel Five, wanting to send a crew over to interview us. I was sure she wouldn't be the last to call. Kate Vare had probably personally talked to some media people, to put more of a squeeze on Robin—and on me.

I wished my friend Lori Pope still worked at the *Republic*. She was a real cops reporter, the kind that dug into cases and built sources inside law enforcement. I had been one of those sources. She would give information back, and I needed it now. But Lori had been laid off with many of the most experienced reporters and now the newspaper mostly rewrote the press releases from the police public information officers. Most of the paper was that way now. I continued to subscribe out of some misplaced belief in the written word and the free press.

Phoenix was increasingly a freak show. Ted Williams' head was frozen in Scottsdale, waiting for the day the slugger could be regenerated. Unfortunately some employees decided to use his noggin for batting practice. The richest man in town didn't support the arts, but he spent money to try cloning his dead dog. A disgraced former governor remade himself as a pastry chef. It was a city where a man left his wife by killing her and his children and then blowing up his suburban house, where a woman cut up her lover and left him in a dumpster. The "Torso Murderess."

What a town. A top city official climbed on top of his Mercedes at high speed and went surfing on Camelback Road, until he and the car hit a wall. It was where retirees sold pot to support their gambling habits and Jenna Jameson, the porn star, was a local businesswoman. Up in Sedona, a self-help guru baked his clients to death in a sweat lodge. Now, a severed head delivered via FedEx. Just another day in paradise and we were part of the freak show. My hometown. The machine clicked off, its red light merrily blinking.

Robin stood before me, watching.

"We're not answering the phone or the door. We have some decisions to make."

"Are we going to Peralta's?"

"Is that what you want to do?"

"No." Her hands were fists. "I know you don't believe me, but I never meant to bring this onto you, especially not after what you've been through. I can't go to Lindsey Faith, I know that…"

"How?"

"I just know her, David. So maybe I should just go. I have some friends in San Francisco."

I stopped her, mindful of Lindsey's charge. "Please. Stay."

"Can we make a stand here, at the house?"

I thought about it. Maybe we could. Much would depend on what happened next.

"We can try. We have some work to do."

We went back to the garage and lugged out a six-by-four-foot plate of one-eighth-inch thick sheet steel. It had been back there as long as I could remember and it was a miracle it wasn't hiding a black widow nest. The deadly spiders, as well as scorpions, had made a big comeback in the years since DDT had been outlawed. The steel plate was just dusty and edged with rust. I wiped it down and we slowly moved it into the house, working up a sweat trying not to gouge the hardwood floors. I directed Robin to help me situate it inside the guest-room closet. Houses built in the 1920s lacked the giant closets of today. This one was maybe five feet deep. But it was wide enough that I could lean the steel plate up against the outer wall. The plate stuck out past the doorjamb maybe two feet, with enough room to slide around it and close the door.

"What's that all about?"

"It's your safe space," I said. "If something goes down, get in that closet, and hide behind the steel plate. Take your cell. You'll have enough time to call the police. The plate should protect you if they start shooting through the closet door." At least I hoped it would.

She listened with her tough-girl face on, but her eyes were anxious. "And if they open the door?"

I walked her into my bedroom and showed her the .38 Chief's Special. "Do you know how to shoot?"

She opened the cylinder, saw its five chambers were empty, clicked it back into place, and pointed the compact revolver toward the wall, dry-firing it several times. "Yes."

Full of surprises, my sister-in-law.

"When Kate Vare comes back, she's going to go at you harder than ever. You can't tell her about taking the dog tags. Ever. Understand?"

She said she did, and asked if I had .38 ammunition.

Chapter Eight

The next week passed dreamlike, uneventful. I was evermore conscious of how the days slipped by, time brutal. Robin and I agreed to some house rules. We wouldn't go out. Move the Prelude into the garage, with its entry on the alley. Let the mail and newspapers pile up. Turn on the lights only in the interior rooms, such as the study and the kitchen, where I tacked up a blanket over the windows that looked into the yard.

We went through the tamales and almost all the cans of soup and frozen Lean Cuisines. I cooked breakfast until we were out of eggs. With the blankets on the windows, the room seemed like a scene out of a World War II blackout. There was nothing to be done about the big picture window in the living room, so we avoided it and kept the lights off. I called out an alarm service and made an appointment to install a system that we couldn't afford.

Fortunately I had bought three large bottles of Beefeater before we became shut-ins. Robin, a wine drinker, began downing martinis. I had to start rationing olives. We drank the house's only bottle of champagne on New Year's Eve and I tried not to get nervous when I heard the fireworks. Robin would get in foul moods because she couldn't go running but was otherwise decent company. She was not an omnivore reader, and unfortunately we had only two real art books: The Phoenix Art Museum catalog—the museum director and his wife lived around the corner—and an Edward Hopper album. So Robin drank each book dry, then watched television, searched for jobs on the Internet, and listened to her iPod while I tried to read. My history books had always been a refuge—my history porn, as Lindsey called it. They were less so now. My mind wandered.

The street seemed unchanged from before the ghastly FedEx delivery. The usual neighborhood walkers went by at their usual times. Two houses down, the winter lawn was coming in nicely. Cypress was dark and normal-looking at night. No drive-by shooting through the window. No Molotov cocktail into the carport. It almost made me think the worst was over. That we could do this and survive.

At night, I made sure the guns were in easy reach. Sleep evaded me and I lay in the big bed, sure I was going to die within the next seconds. Almost all of my adult life these panic attacks had hit me when I was alone and things were quiet. They had kept me from writing more, from playing well with others when I was on a faculty, probably helped take away my chances for tenure. Sharon Peralta had diagnosed me. Knowing what they were barely made it better. My heart thumped hard and fast against my chest. My breathing was constricted. I was terrified about the next minute and every second within it. They only came in the quiet times. I hoped for a call from Lindsey in the middle of the night, when we might talk soul-to-soul as in the old days, but it didn't come.

We talked every couple of days on a regular schedule. She couldn't talk about her work. She didn't ask about the house or her gardens. She wanted to know how Robin was doing. On the most recent call, I asked her again to let Robin come to D.C. Then I demanded it and we had a bad fight. It was like all our fights of late, intense and open-ended. She refused. "You're to blame," she said at one point, as if it were an all-embracing state-ment. Maybe I was. I stayed up all night rewinding and playing our words in my head. The pilfered evidence sat in the bottom of my desk drawer, a worthless riddle and my own culpability in concealing evidence.

Finally, I started taking a chance and slipping out the back at night, making a slow walk around the block, watching for the unusual. More than once, I saw a coyote running along Third or Fifth Avenues. They had come into the city as sprawl destroyed their habitats. From the street the house looked unoccupied. One night around three I saw a Chevy parked mid-block with two men in it. It had rained again and I could smell the special scent of the wet desert soil. My body stiffened and I reached for the comfort of the Colt Python's custom grips. I didn't know if they saw me, but I got close enough to pick out the license plate. It had the first three letters that an insider knew belonged to Phoenix Police undercover units. So Vare was keeping the house under surveillance, at least some of the time. It didn't give me much comfort. Otherwise, Vare stayed away.

The media moved on, to a gang rape out in the suburbs that occurred after a high-school dance, to the shooting of a police officer in the white suburb of Gilbert, reminding readers and viewers that "things like this don't happen here." The implication was that they did happen in the city, where the brown-skinned people lived, where severed heads were delivered right to your doorstep.

Peralta left office without talking to the media. The new sheriff immediately announced he would begin sweeps to arrest illegal immigrants. Peralta had focused on the smugglers that abandoned the immigrants to die in the desert, or held them hostage—sometimes a hundred in a house—until relatives paid to set them free. He had worked with the state attorney general to go after the electronic fund transfer services such as Western Union. The bad guys used them to move ransom money.

Violent crime in the areas policed by the county was at twenty-year lows and the jails were well run. He had put Bobby Hamid in prison. Mike Peralta had been the best sheriff in the county's history, better than "Cal" Boies—Peralta never used his deputies to sway an election—better even than Carl Hayden, who went on to be one of the longest-serving senators in American history. He stood for, as I heard him say in one campaign speech, "tough law enforcement and simple justice." In the end, the only thing that seemed to matter was his opponent's pledges to "stop illegal immigration." "What part of illegal don't you understand?!," one of his campaign signs read. I wondered who did the landscaping at the new sheriff's house in Fountain Hills. Now he'd probably use inmates.

By the end of the week my beard was coming in nicely. I hadn't worn one since I had joined the Sheriff's Office. I awaited word from the university, wondering what it would be like to teach again, what students were like now. I had seen some of the classrooms. They had high-tech lecterns with a microphone and a computer dock for PowerPoint presentations and all sorts of new media. I didn't need that. Just give me some willing minds. I wondered if I would have to take Robin to class with me. I wondered if I would be endangering the students as long as this case remained open. Some times I lay awake and pondered whether Jax could really be the killer they said he was. Most of the time I fought to keep my mind off the events of last year, especially the late summer when the dreadful heat lingered. Sometimes the bedroom seemed so large that I would shrink to nothing and float away.

If Jax was really involved with the Sinaloa cartel, and Robin was being targeted, there really wasn't a damned thing we could do. That would have been my reaction if I were just watching our lives from the outside. The cartels controlled entire states in Mexico. Even the Mexican army couldn't stand against them. Thousands had been murdered down there. A classroom of kids had been massacred in Juarez recently, wrong place wrong time, but that showed their reach. It was only a matter of time before they reached across the border in a big way.

A battering ram through the old front door followed by an all-out assault. A bomb in the car. Not a damned thing you could do. I knew all this. And I didn't really care if they killed me. That was the truth. For the first time in my life, I didn't give a damn. I was at peace with it, in fact. But I had someone to look after. That was a knot in my stomach. At least this reality made the panic attacks go away. And I was determined we would survive.

After a week, the cabin fever was high enough that I took a chance. We snuck out at ten p.m. in the Prelude and went to the Sonic on McDowell just east of Seventh Street. I couldn't chance a sit-down restaurant, but this seemed as safe as we could make it: well lit, on a major artery with an escape route. I made Robin wear the protective vest under her hoodie. She ate a foot-long cheese Coney and I had a Supersonic cheeseburger and a diet cherry Coke.

Two spaces away sat a Toyota holding a plump woman with long red hair and a little girl with brown hair. The little girl was leaning on mom's shoulder as she ordered. She yelled and started crying. For much of my life, screaming children were like a dental drill in my brain. I mellowed in recent years. It was a strange evolution. The little girl was out too late. She was tired and cranky. I could sympathize. Her hair was wavy, unlike her mother's straight hair, and her face was angelic even in its tantrum. Now when I saw such scenes I just said a silent prayer that the child would be treated well and have a happy life.

"David."

I turned back to face Robin and my half-finished burger.

She said, "Roll up the window. I'm cold."

So we listened to the muted Sonic sound system play old hit songs, and we laughed and made light conversation in the fashion of people who had been through recent trials. My sympathy for her loss grew. My eyes continued to sweep the parking lot and the street, but our only other company was a group of six high school girls in mini-dresses, sitting on the benches and talking to one another. They were slender and mostly Hispanic, with two Anglo girls. I wondered about their stories.

We turned west on McDowell and the dash clock read ten forty-two.

The bump from behind was sudden. The car had come out of nowhere, and at first I thought it might be a fender-bender. It was a low-slung import with glowing purple paint. Traffic was light so I wondered, just for a few seconds, how the driver could have rear-ended us. Maybe he was drunk. Then I saw four doors open and men pile out. I could see guns in their hands.

My foot slammed into the floor, and after a brief seizure where we just sat there waiting to be killed, the old Honda leaped ahead. I ran the red light at Seventh. The oncoming pickup never stopped and I could see the Ford F-150 grille coming into the side window. I got more power out of the engine just in time and as we passed Safeway the speedometer needle was resting on eighty.

"What happened back there?"

"They had guns. Climb in the back seat and lie as low as you can."

Her long legs slid against me as she moved between the seats. She disappeared from the rearview mirror. Unfortunately, the purple car was right on my tail. I swung south on Third Street and accelerated again, then ran the red light at the ramp to the Papago Freeway. The car bumped down hard and I wished I had unloaded the boxes from the trunk. I kept the pedal on the floor and we sped down the ramp to the wide, depressed highway, the tachometer in the red. I had the Python on my hip and wished I had brought the Five Seven. There was no tactical solution if I chose to take them on. They had automatic weapons in that car. I had six rounds and two Speedloaders of ammunition.

The purple car ran up behind and came over into the next lane. It was a Kia. The black-tinted back window came down and a gun barrel came out. I slammed on the brakes, fighting the Prelude as it shuddered, and pulled to the right. My speed dropped in half to forty, and I heard the tires scream behind me. The Kia shot ahead momentarily. It lacked a license tag. That came from a forward glance I made while trying to watch the five lanes of freeway I was trying to thread. The back of a semi came within inches of the front bumper, then I slid into a slot between two more trucks, changed lanes again, and hit the Sixteenth Street exit. A cascade of horns followed my moves. I thought I heard a collision behind me. Where the hell was a cop when you needed one?

"David?"

"Stay down."

I swung south on Sixteenth and blew past Roosevelt doing seventy, swerving between cars. Unfortunately, the rear view gave me no peace.

"Fuck."

I don't know how he crossed that many lanes of freeway after overshooting me by ten car-lengths, but the purple car was a block behind, the streetlights making it glow. The driver was expert. And determined. I unholstered the Python and set it on the seat.

Shooting the driver might slow them down.

Then I hit on a better plan.

Phoenix's traffic lights are generally set so that if you do the speed limit, you'll hit green. So I doubled the speed limit and went effortlessly through Van Buren, Washington, and Jefferson, then crossed the railroad yards on the narrow overpass. Our pursuers easily matched me and bumped us twice. But I kept changing lanes. He wasn't going to get alongside, or get ahead and pull a PIT maneuver: Tactical ramming.

All I needed was one more intersection and in a few seconds Buckeye Road flashed past. Susie's Mexican food was closed and dark. Another half mile and I turned right into the central city precinct of PPD. It was close to shift change and cruisers were coming and going. Scores of marked units were parked and off-duty cops were walking to their civilian cars. The Kia continued on south, not changing speed.

They knew they'd get another shot.

It took a long time before my heart rate dropped down or before I would allow Robin to get in the front seat. It took even longer before we ventured out, behind a police SUV heading north.

"Aren't we going inside? Report this?"

I said no. I had no license tag or decent description of the suspects, and I didn't want to spend the rest of the night in Kate Vare's clutches. I followed the PPD unit all the way to Roosevelt. It was one a.m. and no purple car was behind us. At Roosevelt, I turned left and slipped through the dense old Garfield district, then past the darkened art galleries on the other side of Seventh

Street, bumped over the light-rail tracks by Trinity Cathedral, and headed home. I circled the house twice with the car lights off. Our PPD minders were off tonight. The street seemed empty. Then I took the chance of turning down the alley, where we could be hemmed in and ambushed. I kept the lights off. But the only commotion was the barking dog two doors down.

Later, after some time spent on the computer, I lay in bed in a T-Shirt and sweatpants. The Python under my pillow, the Five Seven on the nightstand, and I went through the events of the evening and tried to formulate a plan. How had they picked us up at the Sonic? I didn't see any tail when we had first pulled out of the garage into the alley, then onto the street. Nobody had been watching us; my late-night walks around Cypress told me that. I had missed something, screwed up…what? I lost it in a deep sleep. When I woke up, Lindsey was next to me. But it wasn't Lindsey. It was Robin, curled against me, facing away, with her hair in my face. It was soft and fresh smelling. I wasn't startled and thought about running her out, but I could hear her quietly crying, feel her chest shaking and heaving. I put my arm around her and pulled her closer, felt her warmth radiate against me, and we were both quiet. In the morning I was alone on the mattress and sure I had imagined the whole thing.

Chapter Nine

Kate Vare stood on the doorstep a little after nine. She held a coffee travel mug with the city of Phoenix logo wrapped around it. She said she was there to take the evidence seal off the garage apartment. We could use it again. I led her up the stairs and she pulled the label off the door.

"So this means what?"

"To me, it's misdemeanor homicide," she said. "Asshole-on-asshole crime. Now we have one less asshole in the world. I've got plenty of cases where real people have been hurt or killed."

She was enjoying this way too much.

"And what about Robin? She's a real person."

"If she's telling the truth, we don't have any further questions."

"A beheaded Sinaloa cartel hit man and no further questions?" I stared past her, taking in the view at treetops from the walkway. The air was yellow brown. "What happened to your big media event? Your major case?"

"Things change, Mapstone." She cocked her head and looked up at me. "Do you see any media? I don't see any media. Meanwhile, we've got a new round of layoffs coming."

"I'm sure Wal-Mart will hire you."

"Oh, I'll be around," she said, sipping her coffee.

So I told her about the chase the night before with the Kia. She shrugged.

"Did you file a report?"

I shook my head.

"Maybe it was a robbery attempt." One eyebrow went up. "Maybe you imagined it all. You look fine now. So if you're worried, file a report. Meanwhile, if Ms. Bryson remembers anything she wants to tell us, call me."

Vare turned like a figurine on a music box and stalked away. I swear she was smiling.

"She's told you the truth." Mostly. "Do your damned job, Kate!" I spoke to her back, which disappeared into the house.

I spent the day writing a grant proposal, to fund a history I wanted to write of Phoenix. If I was going to make my re-entry into academia, I needed to publish again. And the histories of the city were lacking. Brad Luckingham's book left out so damned much and VanderMeer's wasn't even in print any longer. I fretted about my future. Every job was being chased by six unemployed persons, and the competition was much greater among people with advanced degrees in the humanities. The situation was even worse in Phoenix, by far the largest city with only one real university. I hated to be at the mercy of ASU. Although I had gone there as an undergrad, I had long since moved on. But I really needed this job. And they had come after me, several high-ranking folks urging me to apply for the job after Peralta lost the election. By the end of the day, my eyes hurt from so much computer time. Robin did yoga in the guest room and stared out at the interior courtyard, saying little.

In the afternoon, she wanted to know about the family photos on the bedroom dresser. There were my grandparents in black-and-white, around the time they married: 1912, when Arizona became a state. They looked pleasantly unsmiling at the camera, he in his narrow tie and coat, she with raven black hair and wearing a high-necked blouse. The mother and father I never knew were in several photos, my father a surprise baby born to grandmother when she was in her thirties, when they didn't think they could have children. One picture showed him in the war, in his fighter pilot's jacket and a P-51 Mustang behind him. "Dashing," Robin commented. All these people looked impossibly young. Another photo: my parents and me as a baby, taken a few weeks before they flew off to Denver and never arrived. I told her stories that didn't cut too deep.

"You're lucky to know your past," she said. "I don't know anything about my dad. I only knew Linda's mother a little, we were on the road so much." Linda being her and Lindsey's mother, always referred to by her first name.

She sighed and looked at the pictures. "When I was sixteen, one of Linda's alcoholic boyfriends burned down our garage. All the family photos were lost. You should have seen Lindsey Faith. She was the beauty. I was the ugly duckling."

"I doubt that," I said. "I wish I would have asked more when my grandparents were still alive. Grandmother knew the entire family history."

"So no brothers or sisters," she said. "What about other family?"

"My grandmother had a sister. She had a beautiful acreage on Seventh Avenue, when it had irrigation ditches on either side and big trees. But she died in 1976."

"God, you really are alone."

I sprang up and dug into the closet. "Take a look at this." I showed her a scrapbook that Grandmother had kept, page after page of old postcards from Phoenix in the 1930s and 1940s. One showed a narrow Central Avenue lushly bordered by palm trees and manicured grass. Other postcards were from places they had visited, plus miniatures of the labels that went on the citrus crates that were shipped out when this was a farm town. "Arizona Beauty." "Big Town Grapefruit." "Desert Call." "Westward Ho." "Kathy Anne Melons." All were colorfully, lusciously illustrated in the style of the day.

I told her about the rich agricultural valley this had once been, even when I was young. We grew oranges, grapefruits, lettuce, cabbage, summer squash, tomatoes, beets, strawberries, cucumbers, watermelons and more. Just add water to the alluvial soil of the Salt River Valley and almost anything could flourish, especially with the ingenuity of our farmers and the water from our mighty dams and canals. Phoenix had one of the nation's largest stockyards and major packinghouses. We shipped our produce all over the nation in long trainloads. It had almost all been lost to tract houses and shopping strips. Without a ten-thousand-mile supply chain, this city would starve. I was grateful my grandparents hadn't lived to see it.

"What's this?"

She pointed to a post card showing long red, pink, and white rows of flowers, framed by palm trees and the South Mountains. I told her about the Japanese flower gardens that once ran for miles along both sides of Baseline Road. The way the north side of the flower fields swept down toward the city, interrupted by citrus groves and ranches in what was then a largely rural south Phoenix. How my grandparents took me down there most Saturdays, were we would buy cut flowers for the house from one of the simple tin, open-faced buildings facing what was then a two-lane highway.

"It's so beautiful," she said. "And they plowed it all under to build houses and apartments. I can't believe it."

Neither could I.

The pictures and the postcards entranced Robin. I left her and she spent two hours with the scrapbook.

As the evening advanced to ten, I told her I was going for a walk and to stay in her room. I set the newly installed alarm and didn't want her to come out and trip the motion detectors. She said to be careful. It was midnight in Washington and Lindsey hadn't called. She had never gone three days without calling.

I dressed in black and had the Python on my hip. I took the alley west to Fifth Avenue to avoid rousing the dog. The night was chill and the air tasted dusty. It was so quiet I could hear a train whistle from the yards over at Nineteenth Avenue, nearly two miles away. Instead of walking around the block as I had done before, I walked to Vernon, two blocks north, then moved fast back to the east, popping out of the pedestrian entrance in the wall that closed off the street near Central. The bell and whoosh of a light-rail train went by. I cut back down to Cypress and came in from First Avenue, moving toward the house from the block to the east. I had made a wide circle around our house, the better to see the perimeter.

The pickup truck sat against the north curb, near the far corner. It was a compact job, dark paint, and it was occupied. As I got closer, I could see an arm dropping out of the driver's side with a glowing cigarette. Closer, near the house where the state appeals court judge lived—he and his wife had a musical group on the side—I made out the tag and memorized it. It was not law enforcement. Whoever was in the truck had a perfect view down Cypress to our house, and could see if we drove out the alley onto Third Avenue. It was also parked in front of the two corner houses that were for sale and unoccupied—a great spot if you didn't want to attract attention. This was how they had picked us up last night.

I counted on two advantages: my quiet old Nike's, and the hope that he would be staring ahead. I had other hopes: that he might be bored and careless. But you can't live on hope. I pulled the big Colt and walked with the barrel pointed down.

As I got to the left rear of the truck he dropped the butt on the street, where it joined a dozen of its colleagues. Almost immediately, a match flared in the cab, illuminating only one occupant, then it went dark and the hand flicked it out the window.

"Smoking'll kill you."

He still had the cigarette in his mouth and his arm outside the cab when I got to his side. I stood just behind him so he couldn't really see me, just like they teach about handling a traffic stop. The difference was that I had the Python's barrel pointed at his head. He turned and bumped into it with his cheek.

"And so will I. Put your right hand on the dash."

My finger was on the trigger guard, but he didn't know that. I didn't want to accidentally blow his head off. I was taking a chance, though. If his left arm had been inside, he had the opportunity to open the door suddenly and knock me to the ground. I could almost see the thought bubble above his head.

"Keep your left arm where it is."

He looked Hispanic and about my age, with a large head and black hair combed straight back. He was wearing jeans and a checked short-sleeved shirt, with tats on his lower arm. He slowly tossed the smoke out the window and laid his hands on the dashboard.

"Where's your weapon?"

I nudged him again with the barrel and he said, "Right on the seat beside me. I'll be happy to show you if you're willing to fight like a man."

"Hand it out. Use your weak hand."

He started to move his left and I cracked his temple with the barrel.

"You're a lefty, asshole. I saw you light the cigarette."

"Chingaso."

"With your mother, asshole. She liked it a lot. Hand out the gun very slowly. Keep your left hand where it is."

The gun came up and I took it. A black TEK 9, one of the old gang-banger weapons of choice, no doubt converted to full-automatic fire. I moved back two steps, clicked on the safety, and tossed it on the asphalt behind me. The street was empty and the lights were off in most of the houses. No cars even came by on Third Avenue.

I pulled on the door handle.

"Out and on the pavement, very slowly."

He obliged grudgingly, dropping to his knees, then lowering himself face down with his arms straight out. He knew the routine from much experience. Everyone should have a career, and here was a career criminal. A chain dangled down from his neck holding a silver cross. I did a quick pat-down, finding nothing but a wallet. I stuck it in my pants.

"You robbing me?"

"Sure. What are you doing here?"

"Smoking."

"Why are you watching the street?"

Suddenly the streetlights went sideways and I was on my back, barely avoiding the hard pavement with the back of my head. His bulk was immediately on top of me. I fought to breathe as he grabbed with both hands for the revolver. Stupid, stupid rookie mistake, standing too close, not watching—he had reached for my ankle and pulled me down. He was strong. Years doing weights in prison will do that. And I only held control of the Python in one hand. I had just enough strength to toss it out of his reach.

He tried to scramble for it and that's when I brought my knee into his balls. I felt a satisfying fleshy connection and he made an "oomph" sound. It gave me enough time to flip him over and slam the heel of my hand into his nose. I heard cartilage snap and a glob of blood spurted in his upper lip. I sprang up and got hold of the Python again, turning around in time to see him crawling for the TEK 9.

"Don't!" I was panting and bouncing on the balls of my feet, adrenaline sending me ten feet in the air. He looked back and studied me.

"You had to think about it," he huffed, pain pinching his face. "That's the thing about guys like you. You hesitate. You think."

I was in a two-handed shooting stance now, his upper torso lined up in the Python's precision sites, three feet away. I said, "Don't make me think too long."

He put his head on the street and brought his legs up, giving in to the agony down in his crotch.

"Motherfucker."

I took the opportunity to kick him in the side.

"Fuuuck! I'm filing against you, homes, police brutality."

So he knew who I was. This was no small-time burglar or car thief prowling the neighborhood.

"Guess what, genius. I'm not a cop anymore. I'm just another concerned citizen." His head rose and he watched me closely. His pupils seemed to dilate despite the streetlights.

"I'm asking you again: Why are you watching the street?"

His bit his lip to fight the pain. "You know the drill, homes. I got nothing to say."

"You sound like somebody using dialogue out of an eighties gang movie." I forced myself to ratchet down the barely controlled hysteria inside me. I had almost lost my gun. "You're not coming back here. And I want you to send a message to your keepers, asshole. The woman who lives down the block didn't have anything to do with anything."

"Says you."

"That's right. And you're going to have to take my word for it. She doesn't know anything. She doesn't have anything. She hasn't crossed anybody. No *venganza*." Revenge. "Your friends didn't even kill the right guy. They killed an innocent civilian and the cops aren't going to just drop it."

"Not what I hear," he muttered.

Now how did he know that? I poked his sore side again with my shoe and he winced.

"You kicked me in my balls, man!"

"You're lucky I didn't just shoot your ass."

"Next time, homes. Next time. I won't hesitate."

Now I was running cold, just like training had taught me. I kept him in the gun sight. "There's not going to be a next time you like, homes. You people aren't going to be the only ones watching. I'm going to be watching. You won't know when or where. I'm going to be watching this street, and if I have to blow away some felons, nobody's going to bother me about it."

"If you have the *valor* to pull the trigger."

"You don't want to find out. Better for everybody that we just drop it."

"They won't drop it, *chingaso*. They never do."

"If they don't, *Estás chingado, hombre*." You're fucked, man.

My legs were going stiff, but I went on with it. "Now, you be a good messenger boy and get the hell out of here." He raised himself with difficulty and fell back into the driver's seat. I said, "If I see your hand come out of that window, I'll kill you. If the truck turns around and comes at me, same deal. Drive away. Don't come back."

He looked at me with sad eyes.

"My wallet..."

"*Adios*, asshole. I might need to know your name so I make sure it gets on the street that you talk to cops."

He thought about it. He thought about it again. Then he sighed, closed the door, and started the truck. It drove slowly down to the corner and turned north.

I picked up the TEK 9. He also left his matches. The matchbook was yellow and said Jesus Is Lord Pawn Shop, with an address on Bell Road. I put them in my pocket and slowly walked home, my butt and lower back aching, my nerves drained. When I crossed Third, I could make out a pair of taillights several blocks past the traffic circle at Encanto Boulevard, moving slowly away.

Inside the house I sank gingerly into one of the leather chairs in the darkened living room, sweat against my chest, and my hands shaking so badly I had to put them under my arms. Nausea flooded my middle. I looked at the bookshelves in an urgent attempt to hold onto something steady: the shelves with grandfather's books and mine, lifetimes of reading and reflection. It was a few minutes before I could will my legs into the bedroom, where I stowed the TEK 9, replaced the Python on the nightstand, and got into my sweatpants for bed. I missed sleeping in the nude. I missed a lot of things about my old life. I sure as hell didn't know the person who had just done that takedown on the street. Was I willing to shoot the banger? Yes, I was.

An hour later I was still lying flat on my back staring up at the ceiling. Robin's door opened quietly and I watched her pad across the landing that separated the two bedrooms. She wore boxer shorts and a T-shirt. Her nipples were obvious even in the semi-darkness. I let her climb into the bed and lie down next to me, resting her head on my shoulder. Neither of us said a word. She put her hand on my bare chest and I fought any feeling. I did not know myself or what I was capable of. It was nearly three a.m. in Washington. I turned away from her and this time I was the one crying while she held me close, her front to my back. I tried very much not to notice the contour of her body against mine, head-to-toe, or to remember how it felt that night on the landing when we were both naked holding onto each other, or how it had felt the other time, when she first came into our lives. My wedding band weighed on my left hand, the room grew cooler and after a long time it dissolved into sleep.

Chapter Ten

The man who stood before me at the Jesus Is Lord Pawn Shop was a middle-aged Anglo with short, gray hair and skin the color and texture of a scrubbed potato. The Arizona sun will do that. His face was unremarkable except for the fact that he lacked one eye. He didn't wear a patch, frosted glasses, or any kind of prosthetic. Instead, his eyelid hung half-open like a stuck garage door, inviting you to stare into the cavity beyond. His good eye was yellow. He was at least a hundred pounds overweight, which was accented by the tight T-shirt encasing his folds of flab. The front of the shirt proclaimed in yellow capital letters, PEACE THROUGH SUPERIOR FIREPOWER. The butt of a revolver stuck out of his shoulder holster.

"Colt Python?" I asked.

"One of my faves, bro."

One can always find common ground.

He stood behind a display counter that ran what looked like a third the length of a football field. It contained every firearm goodie I could think of and quite a few I had never even seen. The old days of a reliable few brands and types of revolvers and some nine-millimeters were long gone. The pistols under the glass were varied and bad-ass looking, plenty of semi-automatics, and a couple that looked like pistol-sized shotguns.

Behind him was a wall of shotguns and assault rifles, as well as another low counter stocked with ammunition. When Barack Obama was elected president, there was such a run on

Phoenix gun shops that even the cops had a hard time finding ammo. They obviously didn't look here. Around me was the equivalent of a big-box gun store, with tables and shelves full of holsters, magazines, Speedloaders, scopes—every accessory a shooter could want. Combat knives were abundant in another display case. Overhead signs marked each merchandise area. It was the largest gun store I had ever seen, exuding the vibe of a porn shop crossed with a hardware store.

The sound system was playing tunes from the seventies. "Brandy" was on at that moment, and I cursed to myself—now I'd have it in my head for a week or more.

The spaces on the wall that didn't contain firearms held a large American flag hung horizontally and a six-foot-long stained wood plaque reciting the Second Amendment. Bumper stickers also abounded: Illegal aliens SUCK, Stop the Invasion, Every Juan Please Go Home, and Illegal Alien Hunting Permit among them.

"I see you have good taste, too." He eyed the Python on my hip. "May I?"

Never give up your gun, Peralta taught. The night before I had almost carelessly lost it. Now I unholstered it, opened the cylinder, and dropped the shells into my palm. Then I handed it across the counter to him.

He snapped the cylinder back in, pointed it at me. "Bang!" He laughed with a strangely high-pitched voice, like a boy soprano, and his belly tectonically undulated the folds of his T-shirt. His bad eyelid fluttered then froze again grotesquely in place.

"You're not the jumpy kind, huh?"

"You just caught me on a slow day." I watched him evenly. He examined my gun.

"Nice action. You've taken care of it. Want to sell it?"

I told him no, which was a shame, he said, considering they weren't made any more and he'd give me top dollar.

"Shoot it much?"

"Every now and then. Helps me relax."

"You bet your ass." He handed the gun back to me. "I'm Barney."

"David."

We shook hands. He was one of those guys who wanted to hurt you with a handshake. I returned the grip back at the same intensity. He appraised me freshly with his good eye and the handshake ended.

"So what can I do you for?"

"Never been in. Looks like a great store. I had a friend pass on one of your matchbooks and I thought I'd check it out."

"I got a hundred boxes full of 'em. Help yourself." He tapped on the open cardboard container of matchbooks by the cash register.

"But you're not a pawn shop?"

"Used to be. But the chains drove me out of it. Everybody's pawning shit, the economy's so bad now, but an independent outfit has a really hard time making it. Anyway, I get better margins on guns. Now, if you're a revolver man, I've got everything your firepower-seeking heart would desire. If you want more, got a special going on Sig Sauer P238 Equinox. Sweetest little concealable you'd ever want."

"They're nice." I knew: Lindsey had one. "I'm just kind of browsing for home defense."

"I got you," he said, poking his eye-socket with a stubby finger. "Like to say to folks, 'I got my eye on you!' " This brought more child-like laughter. "I don't always look like this. Usually have in my glass eye. But last night I went down to this club, see. That one down on Indian School? The Stuffed Beaver, with all the neon out front? Was buying this stripper drinks—Jager shots—and she's never seen a glass eye before. Get it? Seen a glass eye?" I was in the presence of comedic genius. "Anyway, I pop it out and show it to her and she fools around with it and puts it in her mouth and next thing you know, shit, she swallows it! Fuck, that eye cost real money!"

Up until now, he had been speaking in a flat, Midwestern accent. Suddenly, a little Southern came in. "I was fixing to get real mad, started yelling at her, and she turns green and runs to the bathroom. I run after her. Well, kinda wobbled—I was three sheets. I go right into the ladies room behind her, and she runs into one a the stalls, bends over and, hell... Throws up! My glass eye right there in the toilet with all that barf from drinking all day and not eating, guess 'cause she has to keep her figure."

"Not good," I ventured.

"Damned straight. She also heaved up her dentures. Girl can't be more than twenty-five. Pretty little thing. Named Destiny. And she's got false teeth." He sighed. "What can you do? So here I am without my eye."

At least he didn't call himself "Deadeye."

I repeated, "Home defense."

"Got it." Now he was from Iowa or Nebraska again. "Here's this little Kel Tec number back here." He pointed to one of his guns on the wall. It looked like something from a science fiction movie. "Gas piston. Ten rounds, but I can give you a deal on a thirty-round mag. Sweet. Just remember, if you do 'em in the yard, drag the body inside your door. Self-defense. Now, 'course if you're a traditionalist, which it looks like you are, I recommend a Remington 870, twelve-gauge, with a pistol grip..."

While he went on, I nodded, and checked the place out more. It was retail space that had gone through many incarnations. The drop ceiling looked as if it hadn't been replaced since LBJ was president, and it had dark yellow water stains in some spots. At the back of the long room was an alcove and scarred double doors. Still, a new surveillance camera was mounted in one corner, inside a saucer-like cowling that allowed it to swivel to different angles. I watched it as it turned. Also at the back was a mirror, probably one-way glass. He was the only worker visible in the store but I sensed he wasn't alone. I was the only customer, which seemed odd, even if it was the middle of a workday and Phoenix was in its worst recession in history.

"Let me think about it," I said, told him he owned a great store.

"I'm proud of it." He rubbed at his missing eye. "Been out here twenty years and seen what they did to this place. Tax and spend. Open borders. A goddamned invasion. Islamo-fascists coming, too. No wonder people are scared and need to buy guns for home defense. At least we got rid of that spic sheriff."

Something primal inside cocked my muscles to reach across the counter, pull his head down into the glass display case by his ears, and add to his facial deformity. I could have done it before he ever got his fat hand to his gun. I did a quick relaxation exercise Sharon Peralta had taught me. I took a deep, grateful breath. The past was gone and the future was unknowable, even if I couldn't face it. All I had to do was be in that moment. My lungs filled with air.

"You okay, mister?"

"Yeah," I said. "I'm just thinking about how much money I'd like to come spend here."

He smiled wide, showing a set of teeth right out of Hollywood. "Don't let the old lady know. She'll want you to buy furniture or some such shit. But if she's a shooter, bring her by! Got an underground range!"

I thanked him and walked out the door, the laser sensor sounding a loud tone back in the store. From the speakers, Warren Zeavon was kicking in "Lawyers, Guns and Money."

Robin was sitting in the car when I got back. Her hands were covering the Chief's Special that sat between her legs. Today she had refused the protective vest and I hadn't argued.

"Any trouble?"

"Just sitting out in this suburban hell. Maybe that's unfair. Somebody built this, sweated over it, maybe was proud of it. I sat here wondering if anyone could paint this as a landscape… capture the desolation. How small it all is under the sky. I wish I had the talent to paint. I don't, so I studied the ones who did."

"You're not through yet," I said.

She smiled slightly. "What now?"

"Let's sit awhile and watch."

"I've never been on a stakeout. But why are we doing this?"

"Following a clue."

"Why not let the lady cop who hates you do it?"

I shrugged.

"Because she doesn't give a damn. She thinks you're hiding something, and she wants to squeeze you." That's why we sat here. A connection between Jax/Verdugo and the gun store might be tenuous. It might be important. I had contacts beyond Kate Vare. I couldn't protect Robin alone. Maybe I was a fool to think I could protect her at all. *They won't drop it, the scumbag had said last night. They never do.*

Robin said, "Do you believe me?"

"Yes."

I said it with a certainty that I rationally had confidence in. It wasn't because of the nights we had spent side-by-side. I told myself that. The silence lasted long enough for the mood to change.

"You miss the cops, David. You do. Don't deny it."

She smiled wide, making her face beautiful, and starting to resemble her sister. I set that thought aside and pulled across the street into the lot of another decaying set of storefronts, then parked beside some clothing-donation containers. To the south, Shaw Butte and the North Mountains were befogged in the dirty air of three million cars. When I was in high school, Bell Road had been a two-lane highway through a mix of flat desert and used-car lots. The city planners had vowed it would be the northern boundary of Phoenix for decades to come. Now it was six lanes wide and the city limits were many miles farther north. The growth machine had come and gone, a freeway paralleled it a quarter mile north, and Bell had been left seedy for much of its route from Sun City across Phoenix until it became more prosperous-looking near the Scottsdale city limits. Every place changes. I wondered why my city had to change mostly for the worse.

As cars sped by doing sixty, I told Robin about how empty it once was up here. My buddies and I launched model rockets in the empty desert a few miles to the east. "I wish I could have seen it back then," she said. I heard Lindsey, in her former voice, saying, "Tell me a story, History Shamus," and my heart gnawed at my breastbone.

My eyes stayed on the ugly building across the street. The gun store anchored an aging, low-slung shopping strip with a discount smoke shop as the only other tenant. Its sign was gigantic: JESUS IS LORD PAWN SHOP in five-foot black letters against a bright yellow backdrop. Beneath those: GUNS, KNIVES, AMMUNITION. The meek shall inherit the earth but not Bell Road.

We sat for an hour with the windows open, a gentle breeze blowing between us, the winter sun in our eyes. Half a dozen customers came and went, always solitary, middle-aged white men in pickup trucks or SUVs. I engaged in profiling and was not disappointed. For a place whose matchbook was found on a Hispanic banger, this was not exactly an oasis of diversity. One man carried a rifle into the store and came out empty-handed. The others carried out white plastic bags weighed down with guns or ammunition.

Finally, I spoke into the cool air. "We can't keep doing this."

"I know. I want lunch."

"You know what I mean. We're headed for trouble."

"It feels good" She brushed back her hair and smiled at me. "I like it. You do, too. You haven't done anything you have to feel guilty about or confess to Lindsey Faith."

I stared into the pawnshop. It had windows tinted aluminum and bars across them. Small planes flew overhead, coming into Deer Valley Airport.

"Nothing's going to happen unless you want it to." Her voice was even and damnably soothing. "And if it does happen and afterwards it bothers you, that's your hang-up. I decided a long time ago that I don't like to be alone, and I don't have to be, so I won't be. I sure as hell am not going to feel guilty."

"Robin, you're my sister-in-law." I looked at her again, the sun turning her hair to a rich gold color.

"David, we have slept together. Literally. Didn't they do that on the frontier all the time..."

"Not that way."

"Whatever. If you have an erection that persists more than four hours, as they say in the ads." Her smirk was brief. "Things happen between people. Chemistry, passion. Lindsey Faith is

my half-sister and the truth is, your marriage is falling apart."
She put her hand firmly on mine. "Now don't get pissed off.
It's just the truth. You've both been through a lot. When was
the last time you made love to her? When was the last time she
really wanted to make love to you?"

I wasn't angry with Robin. I did fight to keep my throat
from closing off.

"There's a lot about my sister that you don't understand,"
she said.

It ate me up, but I had to admit she was right.

Another pickup pulled in and another white guy got out,
walking with a wide stride into the store. "Anyway," she went
on, "You don't have to worry. I'm not going to fall in love with
you." Her hand left mine. "Which doesn't mean I don't like
you. I do. I love the feeling of your body against mine. I just
don't intend to get under your spell. That would be trouble."
In a different tone, she said, "Check this out."

The long black Chevy Suburban bumped loudly from the
street into the lot and drove straight to the front of the gun
shop. It didn't use a parking space but pulled up just ahead of
the door. Two muscular Hispanic men got out. They weren't
bangers. Both wore suits without ties. The driver did a subtle
scan of the surroundings and then they both went inside. They
moved with a limber, professional gait. If I didn't know better,
I'd think they were cops.

Another half hour passed, enough time for the other customer
to leave. Soon after, the driver came out and opened the back of
the Suburban—it had double doors. Then my new pal Barney
wheeled out a cart stacked with long, thin boxes. The three men
hefted them into the SUV. The operation took ten minutes at
the most, but it was enough for three loads on Barney's cart.
The three men shook hands and the Hispanics sped away. Unless
they were buying ammunition for local law enforcement, they
were definitely not cops. At least not friendly ones.

Chapter Eleven

I took another chance that evening following cocktails. After getting Robin in the guest room and setting the alarm, I walked around the corner to a bungalow on Encanto Boulevard. It belonged to a neighbor who we had over for dinner parties, when we used to have them, and saw at Central Church on Palm Lane, before Lindsey had decided that if God really did exist she hated him. The door opened after the first knock and Amy Preston invited me inside.

She was fair-haired and attractive, in a girl-next-door way, wearing her mid-thirties well. As usual, she was dressed in a conservative pants suit. If asked where she worked, she would say, "the Department of Justice." But she really worked for what I kidded her was the "fun agency": The Bureau of Alcohol, Tobacco, and Firearms. The joke had been spoiled somewhat when the feds added "explosives" to the title.

I met her when she first moved into the neighborhood and had stopped by to ask if a homeless person was camping behind our house. The answer was no—the camper had temporarily bedded down behind the overgrown back yard of a nearby house, owned by an elderly couple whose kids I had gone to school with. But that was how we met. It took a long time to realize that her businesslike restraint was not just because she was the supervisor of an elite federal law-enforcement unit, but also because she was shy.

"David. My God, are you all right?"

I told her I was and took a seat on one of the mission-style chairs in her perfect Pottery Barn living room.

"I guess not completely, since you're packing."

I had the Python under my windbreaker. I said, "An armed society is a polite society."

"Yeah, yeah. I read about what happened. Did you know this…person? The story only said it was an unidentified male."

"It was Robin's boyfriend. You never met him." I turned down her offer of wine. "He claimed to teach at NYU and was in town writing about sustainability. It's the latest fad in academia." I paused. "Unfortunately, it all seems to have been a scam." I continued: Now the cops had an entirely different assumption, all based on the man's ring that I had found in the death house. I described the design.

"El Verdugo." She looked at me thoughtfully. "He's been on the radar for several years." She added, "If he's real. Some analysts think he's an amalgamation of different hired killers, but the myth is more powerful to the cartel."

"The bogeyman."

Her eyes were still. "Something like that."

Amy was circumspect, even though we both worked in law enforcement. At one time, I would have been inclined to think: typical fed. Now I was more willing to accept that she had secrets she had to keep. We didn't talk shop and I had never asked her for a professional favor.

"Are you still staying at home?" she said. "I'm surprised. Robin might be a target—I'm not telling you anything you don't know. PPD's providing protection, I assume."

"I don't count on it. The lead investigator is Kate Vare."

"Ah, Ms. Professional Jealousy. Surely she wouldn't let that get in the way."

"I wish I could say that."

The talk stoked my anxiety about Robin. But she knew the drill: if the alarm went off, she would immediately get in the safe space behind the steel plate, with the Chief's Special, and dial 911. "Tell the dispatcher," I had drilled her, "it's a break-in that is in progress. They respond to those words, 'in progress.' "

Amy sipped from the glass of white wine on the table beside her chair. The calm normality I felt in her house was so at odds with the intensity of our lives on Cypress that it broke my stride, diverted me from my mission. Then I heard Bruce Springsteen's "Tunnel of Love" album softly playing in the background. Just the kind of thing I had banned from my life lately. The Boss sang "Cautious Man" and the weights on my heart swelled. "Weights" was probably the wrong word. They were compartments in which I had placed recent disasters and sorrows — stuffed them full and heavy and tried every waking moment to keep the lids on. It was a learned skill and I was still learning. Fortunately she filled the silence.

"How do you like working for the new sheriff?"

"I'm not going to stay."

I lied. I bent the truth. For the moment, there was no reason for Amy to think I didn't still carry a badge. It was a useful fiction and I could use it for a few more days without getting caught; paperwork traveled slowly down on Jefferson Street. I had used my name and badge number that afternoon to run my scumbag through the NCIC. His wallet had two stolen credit cards and fifteen dollars cash, but his California driver's license was true. And he was a member of La Familia—on parole after doing time for assault and weapons possession, the latest in a long and violent sheet.

"Here's a gift for lighting your backyard grill." I reached into my windbreaker pocket and tossed Amy the yellow book of matches. She studied it all of five seconds.

"Where did you get this, David?"

"Off a banger who was watching the house the other night. He's La Fam. Then I took a little field trip, too. Quite an operation at Jesus Is Lord. Good ole Barney."

"You know you shouldn't be doing this." Her voice assumed a taut, supervisory tone. "If you see a suspicious vehicle, call PPD. This isn't a county case and you're personally involved anyway. I can't believe you did that."

But I did, so I just smiled at her, and let the silence collect between us.

"How's Lindsey taking all this?"

"She's concerned. She's in D.C."

"Already? Well, she'll go far. Fighting cyber attacks is the growing field and she's got the skills."

I didn't go for the distraction. I just watched her and kept my mouth shut.

"Look," she said, "you know Phoenix is the center for people smuggling into the United States. The *coyotes* bring them across the desert and once they're here, they spread out all over the country. Even corporations hire the smugglers to get them to the poultry and hog operations in North Carolina or the packing plants in Nebraska. We're number one in kidnappings and almost all of that is tied into the people smuggling. Now the probability is high that we've become ground zero in the drug trafficking organizations' ongoing expansion in this country. So if La Familia has shown up, it doesn't surprise me."

"And they say we don't have a diverse economy."

She didn't smile. "Local law enforcement is not ready for what's coming, David. That war down in Juarez and Tijuana—it could come here. The people behind their gated communities think this won't touch them. They're wrong."

"But I thought tax cuts would solve everything," I said.

"The thing is, we don't just import and distribute, with all the bodies along the way. We're probably the biggest hub for firearms smuggling back the other way."

"The drug war in Mexico."

"Exactly," she said. "Calderon's offensive has set off a bloodbath down there. The cartels get their guns from here." The Mexican president had promised an offensive against the narcos, and the border had been convulsed with violence. I wondered when we would have a failed state on our southern flank. And the firepower for the bad guys was courtesy of the good old U.S. of A.

I asked her if it was that easy.

She nodded emphatically. "The gun laws are so lax. There are six thousand licensed gun dealers in the border states and we have two hundred agents to police them. Try to get an Arizona jury to convict these gun dealers. Not going to happen."

I listened as she explained the enterprise: American citizens can take the guns across the border—they won't be searched going in. The smugglers hire Americans with clean records, have them buy three or four assault rifles, and take them south. Sometimes they buy at gun shows where there's no requirement to notify the authorities. Other times they use licensed dealers. She said, "Most of the time it moves below the radar. Hundreds of individuals going south with guns. Drugs and money moving north to pay for them. It's very hard to detect."

The Jesus Is Lord Pawn shop didn't seem hard to detect. I described the store.

"I'm aware of it." And that was all she said.

So I detailed what else I saw: the black Suburban, the well-dressed Hispanics, and the large quantity of boxes they loaded. "They were a tad out of place there, to say the least." Springsteen sang "One Step Up." I fought against my guilt and gloom like a man trying to stay standing in a brutal windstorm. Emotional honesty and mordant guitars were not what I needed at that moment. And then it occurred to me. "Mexican cops, right?"

Amy Preston sipped her white wine and shook her head. "You know I can't comment…"

I finished the sentence for her: "on an ongoing investigation."

"Exactly."

I said, "My problem is personal. The people who are watching Robin, the ones who chased us with guns, they're ongoing, too. So everybody needs to understand there's an innocent civilian here and I'll do what I have to do to protect her." My machismo didn't carry me far. I watched her face and ran it all through my head. So after a pause, I added, "I just don't want to get in somebody's way."

But I knew that I already had.

Chapter Twelve

Maybe we should have canceled the trip to Washington. Maybe we should have gone and stayed. I'll never know.

We went and came back, a long weekend. It gave me a chance to wear the good, navy wool topcoat and gray fedora that I had bought years ago in Denver, and of course to see Lindsey. It was cold and the sky was the color of granite for those five days, a nice change for a native Phoenician. As our jetliner took off for home, snow began to fall. By the time we touched down at Sky Harbor twelve inches were on the ground back in D.C.

Before I left, I had asked a retired cop in the neighborhood to keep an eye on the house. He didn't ask questions. A former Marine with a gruff exterior and a great sense of humor, he was now an artist living off his cop's pension. He liked to walk around the neighborhood and keep an eye on things, talk to people. I dubbed him "the Mayor of Willo." As we drove home, I hoped his walks had been uneventful.

On the flight I tried to make sense of things. Some things. Robin's boyfriend had been murdered in the signature style of one of the most notorious gangs anywhere. His identity was a fraud and if the ring was his, it meant he might be a hit man for the Sinaloa Cartel. So far the criminal calculus worked fine. The hit man had gotten crosswise with his employer, who outsourced his assassination to La Fam. The thug watching our house that night had La Familia connections, too. So far, so good.

But why Robin? They sent her an emphatic message via FedEx. Then they tried to ambush us outside the Sonic. What had she seen or heard? We had talked about it so much that I was convinced she really didn't know. And Kate Vare's behavior was strange, too—the case going from priority to back-burner in days. Then there was Deadeye and his gun shop, with Mexican cops, the feds, and my La Fam watcher all drawn to the store up on Bell Road. Maybe the feds had backed Vare off—but if so, why hadn't they tried to contact and interview Robin?

I could make more sense of this jumble than anything that had happened in Washington, where Lindsey was not wearing her wedding rings.

Now we were back under the big sky in time for a spectacular sunset and seventy degrees. People paid the big bucks at resorts for this. We lived here. Of course they were gone by the time summer hell arrived, and most of them weren't targets of a drug cartel. The car flowed into the maze of ramps where Interstate 10, Loop 202, and State Route 51 all came together, then we turned due west as the incandescent pink that rippled across the sky merged into the intense copper glow directly ahead of us.

Robin said, "It's going to be okay, David." And that was the only sound besides the rush of the freeway.

The person was sitting in one of the rocking chairs in front of the big picture window. I could only see the dark silhouette and make out the motion of the chair. I didn't turn on Cypress but instead drove north on Third, my body taut.

I thought about calling the cops. A suspicious person. Let the uniforms handle it. But where would that get us? At best, he'd be a scumbag with warrants out on him, and another scumbag would replace him tomorrow. At worse, he'd show them I.D., get a warning, and go away without me ever knowing who he was.

"If he wanted to kill us, I'm not sure he'd just be rocking on the front patio," Robin said.

"Unless he's a hit man with real *sang froid.*"

I turned and crossed Windsor Street to Fifth Avenue and turned south again. I parked a little past Encanto and gave

Robin instructions. The Python was already on my belt—I had retrieved it from the trunk first thing when we got to the car at the airport. Now I walked slowly toward home, keeping close to the fronts of the houses on the north side of Cypress Street. The sun was gone, replaced by the long, deep-blue twilight that was peculiar to the desert. I hoped it would provide enough cover for me. The sounds and glow of televisions intruded on my senses as I wondered if a neighbor would call the cops on me. But by then I was two houses away. I pulled the Python and carried it straight down, concealed by my leg.

"Howdy."

The silhouette in the chair started. "You…" That was all he got out.

"I want to see your hands." I dropped into a combat shooting stance. My finger was on the trigger and I knew exactly how much pressure the Colt gunsmiths had required to make the hammer and firing pin do their jobs. "Now."

The form didn't hesitate. Two hands shot up straight like in an old Western. It was a small, older man.

"Just take my wallet. I'll get it out for you!" A quavering voice.

"Keep those hands up," I said. "Are you armed?"

"No!"

The house looked fine and the guy didn't seem to have any backup. I moved in closer.

The man in the rocking chair could have been anywhere between sixty and eighty. He was completely bald and clean-shaven. His face looked like a walnut with eyebrows. The walnut was dressed in a loud golf shirt and khaki slacks. His shoes looked expensive. I put my finger on the trigger guard, cocked my arm to raise the gun away, and gave him a quick pat-down. His bones felt brittle. Now I placed him closer to eighty.

"I said you can have the wallet." This time his voice was testy.

"I don't want your wallet. Who the hell are you and why are you sitting in my rocking chair?"

Without taking my eyes off him, I gave a signal to Robin, who had been following me at a distance.

He said, "You're Dr. David Mapstone? I have a business proposition for you."

I let him lower his hands. I holstered the Python and sat in the other chair.

He went on, "You have a funny way of greeting people."

"What's your name and why are you here?" I was not in a hospitable mood.

"Can we go inside?"

"No."

Robin pulled in the car and started bringing luggage into the house. I heard the alarm's warning beep until she disarmed it.

"May I?" He held up a small hand. I nodded. He reached into his shirt pocket and pulled out a business-card case. He handed me the white card. It said: Judson Lee, Attorney at Law.

I told him to come in the house.

"I haven't really practiced law for twenty years. I have a few clients, friends mostly, that I do favors for."

Now he was in the study, in the low armchair, while I sat at the desk. My mind was still back in Washington, where history was everywhere. I hadn't been to the city in years and Robin had never been there. The three of us had walked from the White House to Capitol Hill, around the Supreme Court, the Library of Congress, and the Capitol itself as I told stories. The Capitol dome wasn't even complete when the Civil War broke out and wounded union soldiers were hospitalized inside. The building held a crypt for George Washington, even though he was buried at Mount Vernon. Sam Rayburn's "Bourbon-and-branch water" sessions were held in his basement hideaway, where young LBJ ingratiated himself to the lonely House speaker.

Lindsey seemed distracted, the woman who had once been so moved when I talked history. She walked alongside us, but she didn't really seem to be with us. The National Portrait Gallery entranced Robin; we spent an afternoon there while Lindsey was working. She said little about her new job. Maybe she told Robin more when they had sister time. We ate in restaurants we couldn't afford. The bad economy seemed far away and to a casual observer I was fortunate to be in the company of two attractive women. Lindsey was luminous. Robin, I saw with new eyes. "I'm glad you two are getting along," Lindsey said. I had assigned a guilty cryptic message, of course. But I kept myself tamped down. Mostly.

"Now I have a client who needs your help." The little man paused. "Your special combination of skills, the historian and the deputy."

"I'm not with the Sheriff's Office any longer."

"I know this, Dr. Mapstone. That's why it's a business proposition." He looked at me as if he expected to be offered a refreshment. I sat back and said nothing.

"I'm sure you've heard the name Harley Talbott?"

Of course I had. He was one of the most controversial of Arizonans. Some said he was a great philanthropist. He had his name on a building at the University of Arizona. Others claimed he was a gangster who had been behind the murder of an *Arizona Republic* reporter in the 1970s. Nobody argued that he initially made his money as the biggest liquor dealer in Phoenix.

Lindsey had rented an apartment in the District. She furnished it from Ikea, getting an allowance from the government. Robin slept on the sofa while Lindsey and I shared her new bed. It felt strange, of course. Late at night, I tried to tunnel into Lindsey with compliments—she had cut her hair again, into something called an angled bob; I liked her hair longer but I told her how looked lovely she looked, which was the truth. Her blue eyes were still so stunning against the darkness of her hair. She had new glasses. I told her people in Phoenix thought she was such a star in the new cyber war. Little neighborhood gossip was another light topic, such as whose house had been on the market for two years now, or how the new sheriff was training deputies to be immigration enforcers. My tunneling attempts failed. She said matter-of-factly, "You have a beard."

She wanted to know how Robin was doing. Inside, I wanted to rage "what the hell about us?" I didn't. The crisis back home kept me oddly in control during this visit. I gave her the details of the case but she didn't react much. I felt as if we were back home over the past year, when her silences had grown to terrify me. The closest we came to a fight was when Lindsey once again refused to let Robin stay with her in D.C. The job was too all-consuming right now. She didn't have time to entertain Robin, much less look out for her.

We didn't make love. I lay down in bed nude, like I always used to sleep with her. She slept in her panties, a new innovation. We made out a little but then she patted me on the arm and pulled away, gently but obviously. It was like a switch flipped off. This had been happening for a long time. It made what took place last year more remarkable. Every marriage has its ups and downs. Every marriage has moments when you think you've awakened with a total stranger, when you have moments when you really dislike this person you know that you love. Our story was nothing special. That's what I told myself. But Lindsey's waning interest in sex didn't mean she wasn't interested. I wasn't that self-absorbed. It meant she wasn't interested in sex with me. I lay awake as she slept. On her side of the bed, I noticed a blue pack of Gauloises Blondes. She was smoking again, but not around me. I wondered who else she might share a cigarette with?

In the study now, Robin joined us. Judson Lee stood and introduced himself, holding her hand in a courtly way. "What a beautiful name, Robin," he said. I thought he was going to kiss her hand.

He sat back down and resumed. "This isn't about Harley Talbott, directly. My client is Nick DeSimone, the restaurant owner. He's a great guy. Have you been to his place?" His hands gesticulated in his small lap.

"When I can afford Scottsdale prices."

"Ah." One of the black slashes of eyebrows arched. In the light, his face bore the signs of Scottsdale or Paradise Valley privilege—or rather lack of signs: in spite of its sun-leathered color, it was barely wrinkled. "Well, Mr. DeSimone's grandfather Paolo worked for Harley Talbott when he was young. He was an impressionable kid. Harley was a big personality. Paolo went to prison for Harley Talbott."

"I'm sorry to hear that, but I'm out of the cold-case business."

"This was a miscarriage of justice," he said. "Paolo was no angel at times, that's true. But he had cleaned himself up, started a family. Then this incident happened and he was made to take the fall. His family deserves to have his name cleared."

I told him I could recommend some good private investigators.

"But you're a historian, no? What I'm proposing, Dr. Mapstone, and what my client is willing to pay for, is what you might call family history."

"A family history that clears his grandfather?"

"I can't think of a better person to do it. You solved the murder of the FBI agent, after how many decades? And the Yarnell kidnapping. I know your reputation."

Out of the lawyer's vision, Robin smiled and winked at me.

I told him I appreciated it, but no. I would have my hands full teaching at ASU. I hoped so: I kept waiting to get the final sign-on. Things moved so slowly in academia. Or maybe we would sell the house and move to Washington—I had offered that to Lindsey and she had said no. That was another example where she calmly made a hard pronouncement and ended the conversation, another reason to lie awake. Was she really trying out this job for a few months, as we had discussed? Now the round brown face in front of me kept talking.

"He'd be willing to pay five thousand dollars."

"I can't. But thanks for stopping by. I'm sorry I gave you a scare. We've had some trouble in the neighborhood lately."

"Ah." He stood and shook my hand. "I totally understand. I don't even know anyone who would live down here."

I kept my neighborhood pride tamped down. I didn't tell him you couldn't pay me enough to live in his gated property or mountainside mansion.

He said, "I hope you'll keep my card in case you change your mind. If what I hear about you is correct, this story might really intrigue you."

I walked him to the door, eager to get him out—eager, desperate really, to make drinks.

For the first time in weeks, I put on jazz. Bill Evans, Stan Getz, McCoy Tyner. Coltrane, of course. I drank two martinis and Robin had one. I was drinking too much. It was the least of my problems. Robin opened our last cans of chili, used up the box of crackers, and made me eat something.

When the music stopped, Robin said, "This isn't your fault." There was no question what *this* was. "There's nothing you could have done differently."

"I wonder about that every day," I said.

"I know you do." It wasn't a reproach. Just a gentle commiseration. "There's nothing anybody could have done. Nobody is to blame."

"That may not be what Lindsey thinks."

She didn't respond.

Her face brightened. "If you'll go running with me tomorrow, I'll take you to a bookstore."

"Will you wear the vest?"

"Hell, no." She tried unsuccessfully to pull her hair behind her ears. It fell back, gently framing her smile.

"You are a pain in the ass." I said it fondly.

We sat a long while in the dark living room, until she asked, "Do you want your space tonight?"

I closed my eyes, remembering the previous night, after Lindsey and I had strolled together along the Mall, the monuments grandly lit, the cold sharp. It felt important to try again to make a connection, to find my way back to her. It was a bad idea. I talked and she met me with silence. Until we came back to the Washington Monument, and then she spoke for all of ten seconds.

Lindsey's words were still burning inside me like white phosphorous. The compartments had shattered and now I was carrying the shrapnel. But my body was giving in to alcohol and east-coast time.

I looked at Robin and shook my head. "Come be with me."

Part Two:
The Bitterest Method

Chapter Thirteen

The bedraggled, single-story building on Grand Avenue looked somewhere between sixty and eighty years old, with a single door and a square window on each side. All were covered by bars that might once have been painted. The square structure itself was bleached brown, done in cracking stucco to resemble adobe, and it sat atop the remains of an asphalt lot. It had once been the office to a motel in the golden age of driving, and this was the highway west out of town.

A battered sign on a pole near the street read, very faintly, Easy 8 Auto Court and beneath that, Air Conditioned—It's Cool Inside!, but all the cottages were long gone. Now the office sat by itself, surrounded by barren lots on either side that held dirt and rocks the same color as the building. The only signs of newness were a twelve-foot-high security fence, a couple of halogen lights aimed from the roof, and Peralta's silver Dodge Ram pickup parked in front. The Prelude bumped across the perimeter of the open gate. We got out, went inside, and found Peralta.

"I can't believe this." Those were my first words.

"What, Mapstone? You don't believe in entrepreneurialism? It's the American dream."

He stood from behind an ancient metal desk, came around, and hugged Robin.

To me, he said, "What's that growing on your face?"

A second desk sat at an angle across the room. Two institutional armchairs with green-cushioned seats that might have been new during the Eisenhower administration flanked both, and tall gray metal filing cabinets took up one wall. The floor was old linoleum, the color of coffee with three creams. The sheriff's cigars had augmented the musty smell. Behind Peralta's desk was a framed poster that proclaimed "Diversity." It was meant to look exactly like one of those insipid motivational placards, but the image was of a dozen mean-looking assault rifles laid out neatly on white sand.

"Why are you not in some luxury suite in north Scottsdale?"

"Fake tits on a stick, not my style," he grunted as he sat. To Robin, "Sorry about my language."

She smiled at him.

"And you turned down how many high-powered offers to be corporate chief of security or a national consultant?"

"Thirteen," he said. "But it's a slow job market. I wanted to be on my own."

"You must be crazy. You have a law degree, for god's sake."

He actually smiled. *"Res ipsa loquitur."* The thing speaks for itself.

We sat in the chairs. He didn't look much different. He wore a starched white shirt, red tie, and black slacks, with his usual firearms accessory.

"I'm a private investigator now, Mapstone. It'll be fun. I don't need to make much money. My ex has been very indulgent with her book royalties. But business comes anyway. I just got back from Douglas. Client wasn't satisfied with how the police handled her brother's murder. So I put some fresh eyes on it. Got out and saw a beautiful part of the state."

I repeated, "I still can't believe this. Why here?"

"I like it. The freight trains go by. I'm near my people. You know, I'm just a simple *campesino.*"

"Who went to Harvard," Robin said.

He lowered his head and squinted at me. "Where's your cannon?"

"I'm learning to love the Five-Seven." The semi-automatic was tucked in my jeans, in the small of my back, concealed by my shirt. February, which was once the sweetest month in Phoenix, had come in hot, with today's temperature near ninety. I wished that I had worn a short-sleeve shirt.

"Good." He reached in a desk drawer and slid across a laminated card. "You won't need this once the Legislature makes everything connected to guns legal, but here's your concealed weapons permit."

"But I didn't…"

"Sure you did. I had you sign the paperwork for it the day you resigned." I was irritated but reached over and took the card. He said, "So, give me an update?"

It didn't seem as if there was much to tell. We had survived January, with no more scares, no more watchers sitting on the street at night. Sometimes I had seen a marked PPD unit drive down the street, but it could have been routine patrol. Vare had not even checked in with a phone call. When I called her to get an update, I was told to leave a message. It was, of course, never returned.

He put his elbows on the desk and folded his fingers in front of his face as I talked.

In a way, the lack of action had made the tension worse. But I had kept my anxieties to myself. Robin had become more comfortable, the trauma of opening the FedEx box receding. We held long discussions about the Great Depression—she knew much about the art and artists of the era—and comparisons with things now. She laughed more easily. She had a great laugh, uninhibited and delightfully distinctive. I could find her in a crowd just by her laugh. Although we relaxed some of the house rules—I was getting the mail and newspapers now—I tried not to let us get careless. I wouldn't let her sunbathe outside and she complained that her tan was fading, but the result was quite attractive, at least to me.

…Oh, and I'm sleeping with my sister-in-law…Just that, although sometimes she caresses me in the night and I smooth back her soft hair and when I lie behind her, my front to her back, she knows how I feel about her, unfaithful bastard that I am…I'm not myself. Am I?

The only big news was the email I had received from ASU, blowing me off because of a new round of budget cuts. After all the in-person courting that I received after the election, I lost the job via an email. And it was just to be an adjunct professor, the minimum-wage counter help of academia.

"That must have pissed you off." He leaned back and folded his hands behind his head. The only item of luxury in the entire office was where he sat, in a new executive office chair.

"History teaches humility and skepticism."

"Right. Told you that you couldn't go back to that P.C. shit. And that they wouldn't have you. When Jennifer was at Stanford..." This was his oldest daughter. "...she said to me, 'Why do I have to study something called HIS-story. What about HER-story?'"

I could have pointed out that the word came from the Greek for inquiry and had nothing to do with pronouns, but he was right about the broader issue. I was mad as hell. Hurt, too. Me, the guy who couldn't get tenure at San Diego State University, for God's sake. Now I was rejected for a part-time teaching gig when I knew they were still taking on kids with half my credentials. I felt like even more of a failure, that I let down Lindsey, too. A couple of times I went off on Robin, although I immediately apologized. She accepted my outbursts with surprising equanimity, considering that I always imagined her to be someone who would cold-cock anybody who crossed her. But I had learned new things about her and we had grown closer. She would say, "You're not yourself, David."

Peralta spoke. "I hear you went to visit Amy Preston." He dropped it light as a feather.

"That's true."

"Why were you out there at that gun shop?"

"He misses the cops," Robin chimed in, gently punching my shoulder.

"I don't doubt it," Peralta said. "How'd you like Barney?"

"Barrel of laughs."

"He'd kill you in a heartbeat. Did it occur to you that ATF might have an operation going?"

"Actually, no." I felt the anger start to pulse in my temples. "If PPD wasn't going to protect Robin, why wouldn't I try to follow a lead and get ahead of the bad guys? Kate Vare takes this from a major case to the circular file and I'm just supposed to let it be?"

Peralta stared at me and grunted. Then, "Let's go for a ride."

He didn't ask about Lindsey. But considering he was a good friend of the former Arizona governor who was Secretary of Homeland Security, he probably knew more about my wife than I did. I looked down, feeling my face burn.

The three of us fit easily into his pickup, which sat high off the road. He drove down 35th Avenue past warehouses and the entrances to half-century-old subdivisions of faded ranch houses. This was Maryvale, Phoenix's first automobile suburb, laid down starting in the late 1950s. It was aging badly, like most of the city. This was a hunter-gatherer place, and when one location was used up the people with means simply moved farther out. They left behind thousands of tract ranch-style houses that could never be rehabbed as historic homes, could usually not even justify a home improvement loan. Maryvale would never be gentrified.

In ten minutes, we pulled into a dilapidated shopping strip. But every store was occupied. One sign promised "*celulares*," while another went with a thriving *carniceria*, a butcher store. One of the ubiquitous 99-cent stores held down the far end. Peralta parked directly in front of the *yerberia*.

For most of its history, Phoenix had not been a Hispanic city—that was Tucson, where roots went back to the Spanish conquest, even though an Irishman technically founded the Old Pueblo. Phoenix was the brash newcomer, established by Civil War veterans and assorted fortune seekers in the late 19th century. While it always had a Mexican-American population with its own proud history, the city maintained much of its Southern roots into the early 1960s. Then it started to change with enormous population growth from the Midwest. Tucson was culturally Hispanic and old. Phoenix was mostly Anglo and new.

That distinction started to change with the massive migrations from Mexico and Central America that began in the 1980s. Millions of new immigrants came through Phoenix and many stayed, working in restaurant kitchens, landscaping services, and building houses. If that wasn't enough to destabilize the old Mexican-American population, the city razed many of the poor but historic old barrios to expand the airport. City Hall didn't give a thought to bulldozing Santa Rita Hall, where Cesar Chavez began his hunger strike in 1972. All that was left there now was the Sagrado Corazón church, surrounded by a chain-link fence. The large Hispanic population moved into Maryvale as the Anglos bought new houses on the city fringes. As a result, Maryvale, the whitest of suburbs in the 1960s, was now almost entirely Latino. The same thing was happening all over the older parts of the city except in the Anglo historic districts. If you hadn't been in Phoenix since 1980, you'd be amazed at the Spanish-language signage alone—including that marking the ubiquitous herbal healing stores called yerberias.

This one proclaimed its name in red letters across the plate glass, promising *yerbas medicinales de todo del mundo y articulos religiosos*. Herbal remedies from around the world and religious articles. We walked in to the sound of a long electronic beep, a sweet scent, and found a typical yerberia: long counters backed by floor-to-ceiling shelves of colorful devotional candles, and containers and bottles of all shapes and sizes. Incense was burning in a metal box at the feet of a statue of Jesus.

"This is amazing!" Robin said.

A woman about my age with long black hair and a white blouse ran to Peralta and gave him a hug. Magdalena was the owner, apparently, and introductions were made. She and Peralta conversed in rapid-fire Spanish, of which I could make out about every third word. I heard "pall of death," but realized they were talking about the Phoenix economy. Which was true enough: a city that lived by real estate and low-wage jobs was now slowly dying. Her sons and nephews had worked in construction and now they couldn't find any work. Her daughter had bought four rental houses during the boom and had now lost them all to the bank. She asked Peralta if he wanted a tarot reading and he declined.

"Then come on back," she said. "They're waiting."

We followed her through a door into a small office with cinder-block walls painted baby blue. One man was seated behind a desk and another lounged on a sofa.

"El sheriff!" The man behind the desk came around and shook Peralta's hand with both of his. He was middle-aged and thickset, with short hair, prominent eyebrows, and a faded Mexican eagle tattoo poking out beneath the sleeve of one arm. Again, a long exchange in Spanish, the vowels colored with warmth.

"An old friend?" Robin asked.

Peralta leaned his head toward us. "I put him in prison for ten years."

"And it was the best thing that ever happened to me!" The stocky man shook our hands and said his name was Guillermo Gris. "But call me Bill."

The man on the sofa slowly stood and put his hands on his hips. He was my height, six-two, and his broad shoulders tapered into a slender waist. He was darker than Bill, with an unlined face, and hair so black it had a shine. He wore a blue blazer over jeans and a light-blue shirt.

"Sheriff Peralta."

Peralta said, "It's good to see you again, Antonio." There was less warmth here, unlike with Bill. They spoke to each other respectfully, in businesslike voices.

Bill unfolded two metal chairs and we all sat, me beside Antonio on the sofa. I could see the butt of a pistol under his blazer.

"This is the young lady?" he asked.

"Call me Robin."

He reached over and took her offered handshake, and he didn't look as if he was about to kiss her hand.

Peralta said, "I'd like for you both to tell what's happened the past few weeks."

Robin hesitated and so did I, not knowing either of these men, one of them armed. As often was the case, Peralta was working several steps ahead and not deigning to tell me what was going on. But I nodded to her, and she began with the rainy evening when she opened the parcel. I took over when it seemed appropriate and we alternated back and forth in the retelling. Neither Bill nor Antonio spoke. Antonio stared at the blue wall. Bill smoked a cigarette.

"What do you think?" Peralta directed this at Bill.

He stubbed out the cigarette, exhaled the last plume of smoke, and rubbed his mouth. "These two are alive because they want them to be alive. No other reason."

I asked about the chase on the freeway, the gun barrel coming out of the window.

"They were just fucking with you, letting you know they can do you whenever they want," Bill said.

So much for my heroics.

"Describe the men you saw at the gun shop." Antonio's voice was deep and rich, his English barely accented. I did the best I could, but we had been sitting across a parking lot and a street without binoculars. I couldn't see faces. He gave small, precise nods and said nothing more.

"Sounds all fucked up, though," Bill said. "If La Fam really killed El Verdugo, they probably did it for Los Zetas." He looked at us. "Zetas, the enforcers for the Gulf cartel. Take down a Sinaloa cartel guy."

"Maybe," Peralta said. "But the alliances change all the time. Could have been MS 13; the Salvadorans are spreading fast. Could have been a hit ordered from prison by the new Mexican Mafia."

"Not like back in the day," Bill said. "We always had gangs in this town. Blacks in their 'hoods, and Latinos in theirs. Remember the Pachucos? We had gangs in Sono. Even the sheriff remembers that. He was Sono, too, before his dad made it and he moved out to Arcadia." Bill was referring to La Sonorita.

Like Golden Gate, Cuatro Milpas, El Campito, Harmon Park and Grant Park, it was one of old Phoenix's barrios. Now they were almost all gone. La Sonorita, anchored by Grant Park, El Portal restaurant, and St. Anthony's Catholic Church south of downtown, amazingly survived.

"By the time I came up," he said, "we fought over geographic territory. It wasn't no picnic, you know? The blacks had the Bloods and Crips. We did what we had to do." His voice whooped, "Wedgewood Chicanos, forever!" Then his face turned wistful. "But there was a code, you know? A brotherhood. We were there to protect our own. Now, man, everybody's fighting over every-place. It's all about drugs. The cartels are in it and it's all fucked up. Glad I got out of the life. Glad the big man here got me out."

Antonio looked bored.

Peralta sensed it. "The question is what we're dealing with here? El Verdugo in little Phoenix, Arizona. Don't like the look of that. This is not small-time."

"He wasn't El Verdugo!" Robin said, frustration wrinkling her brow.

"Tell me again how you knew this Jax?" Antonio asked. Robin went through it once more, how they had met at a gallery on Roosevelt Street. Antonio wanted to know which gallery. I could sense tension entering her voice and she started nervously playing with her hair, but she gave the same details I had now heard a dozen times. Was Antonio a cop, FBI, or a P.I. like Peralta? Maybe he was ATF, working for Amy Preston.

"What makes the most sense is that he was killed by the Gulf cartel or by Los Zetas," Antonio said. "Maybe he was on a job here and they found him. Maybe he was trying to leave the life. Either way. Wouldn't surprise me if they contracted it out to La Familia in the U.S. La Familia's gone out on their own since 2006, but they used to have ties to the Gulf organization."

"What about the gun shop?" Peralta asked.

"Zetas were a private army for the Gulf Cartel," Antonio said. "Now the old alliance between the two is falling apart. They're becoming rivals." It was hard to keep things straight. My brain wandered off into analogies with the contending parties of Renaissance Florence, the Guelfi and the Ghibellini, or of the petty German states before the Napoleonic wars. Nothing really changes, except this was all about bloody crime and America's insatiable hunger for drugs and cheap labor.

Antonio's rich voice continued. "Los Zetas recruited from some of the best of the Mexican army. Airborne soldiers. Special forces. The pay is more than those soldiers can make in a lifetime with the government. Now they need weapons, lots of weapons."

"This is the place to get 'em," Bill said.

"It's not enough," Antonio said. "The existing supply is dominated by the Sinaloa cartel."

"So the Gulf cartel or Los Zetas wants its own supply," Peralta said. "Did Vega come out of the Mexican army?"

Antonio shook his head. "Nobody knows where he came from. But he's been connected to at least thirty hits on high-value members of rival cartels. And always, the snake's head is left imprinted on the victim's forehead. Hell of a calling card."

Bill said, "*Alla entre blancos.*" Let the white men settle it.

"No," Antonio said. "This is destroying my country. It's destroying your city."

Robin said, "I can't believe any of this."

I spoke up. "So why are they letting us live?"

Bill looked at me and then at Peralta. He set his meaty hands flat on the desk blotter and shrugged.

After a silence, Antonio coughed. "Good question."

Peralta said, "Give me a minute with these guys."

We left, me reluctantly. Out in the shop, Robin browsed and settled on a thick, tall blue candle that promised "Peace and Protection." She wanted a tarot reading but Peralta appeared and said there wasn't time.

As we pulled away into the street, I wanted to know everything. But also I knew from experience that Peralta wouldn't be pushed. He sat like a pickup-truck Buddha, saying nothing. I settled for a first question, asking about Antonio.

"He's with the Mexican Ministerial Federal Police," Peralta said. "That's the elite national agency. If there's an honest cop in Mexico, he's it."

◇◇◇

We drove back to Peralta's office in silence. The Maryvale ranch houses sat behind low walls and spiked fences that had been added by the new occupants. Bars, usually painted white, covered the windows. The elaborateness of the enclosures seemed an indicator of relative prosperity. This was one of the most dangerous parts of the city, but not because of most people who lived here. They worked hard and played by the rules, as the saying went. Except that they were mostly cut off from the economic and social mainstream, especially now. Who knew where it would end.

But like south Phoenix and the growing footprint of poor, ethnic neighborhoods, Maryvale was a hotspot of gang violence. I knew the basics: at least 35,000 gang members in the metropolitan area, almost all Hispanic and black. Thirty percent of the state's inmates belonged to a street or prison gang. In many cases, the gang involvement went back two generations or more, and the generational nature of the problem was getting worse. My professorial brain wanted to linger on the many social, economic, and political reasons why. Maybe when all this was over, I'd apply for a grant to write about that. But the gun pressing against the small of my back reminded me that this daydream was a luxury I didn't have. The gangs dealt in drugs, weapons, and human cargo. They stole identities and carried out armed robberies. And they fought each other. If a middle-class Anglo civilian like Robin was on their list…

She sat between us and turned to Peralta. "Mike, what is this about the bad guys letting us live? I don't know what that means…"

He crossed the railroad tracks and swung onto Grand Avenue before he replied.

"It means," he said, "that they may want to grab you alive. They haven't been able to do that yet because they know that Mapstone here would go down blazing. He learned one or two things from me."

She stared into her lap, rubbed her hands along the stone-washed denim of her jeans. "They want me alive because they want to do the same things to me that they did to Jax."

Chapter Fourteen

That night we sat in Peralta's pickup again, only this time we were in a parking lot on Central Avenue in south Phoenix. Outside it was pleasantly crisp, in the fifties. All three of us wore light leather jackets. They concealed Robin's protective vest and our firearms. Her unruly hair was tucked in a bun. My cell showed a quarter past ten—a quarter past midnight in Washington. I tried the mental exercise: put it back in the compartment. But the compartment was shattered. The best I could do was look through the windshield and force myself into the moment. From the open spaces, we could look down at the lights of the city and the downtown skyline, which looked entirely different from this direction. Over our shoulders, the red lights of the television towers on the South Mountains blinked in a steady cadence.

I was heedlessly venting my anger over the new sheriff, who was using the department to make large-scale arrests of Hispanics in an effort to pick up illegal immigrants. Why the hell wasn't he arresting the employers—or the Anglos who benefited from cheap yard work or maid service? Where was the arrest of the wire-transfer company executives for helping facilitate human smuggling? Or even bagging big-time *coyotes*? Where was the outrage at the destruction of the traditional Mexican economy by NAFTA and the lack of investment that would benefit ordinary people down there so they didn't have to migrate north? As usual, the working poor suffered. Only the sheriff's "sweeps" were played prominently in the newspapers, along with anti-immigrant letters on the editorial pages. As I went on, Robin elbowed me in the ribs. Peralta serenely ignored me.

"Does this take you back, Mapstone?" The streetlights set Peralta's wide, flat forehead in silhouette. "Summer of '77, when the big gang violence really started. Command and the politicians didn't even want us to use the word 'gang.' Why, Phoenix couldn't have a gang problem. That's what the well-off Anglos wanted to think. Neighborhoods falling apart, but they didn't see it." He chuckled. "Mapstone and I rode together when he was a rookie deputy, Robin. We served warrants down here. I was his training officer."

"And he was a real bastard to work with," I said, staggered again by the passing of time.

"It saved your life," he said.

That was true enough. "You didn't think I'd make it."

"Yes, I did. Robin, you should have seen Mapstone the first time he arrested this hooker we called Speedy Gonzales. He didn't know Speedy was a transvestite."

"Ha. Ha," I said. "And I remember the night you almost single-handedly started a riot at the Marcos de Niza projects…"

"Two young studs still competing," Robin said and laughed.

We were watching the Pete's Fish 'n Chips, which had been here as long as I could remember. The place had survived the building up of south Phoenix, which was once heavily agricultural and bounded by the Japanese flower gardens that ran on either side of Baseline Road. But south Phoenix was also the poor part of town on the other side of the tracks and the Salt River. That part still survived. Pete's had outdoor seating on picnic tables next to the small building, lit by overhead fluorescent lights that cast a white glow out on the otherwise deserted streetscape. At the moment, half a dozen young Latino men sat there, holding court.

"I thought you said…"

"Be patient," he said.

Sure enough, they paraded out to their cars and sped off going north. The picnic tables were entirely deserted for ten minutes.

Peralta shifted in his seat. "Here we go."

A white SUV pulled in, its mandatory spinning hubcaps running. Four black guys stepped out and walked to the order window. They kept a loud hip-hop number playing out of the open windows. Lyrics about the wrong place at the wrong time.

"No colors?" I asked.

"There's less of that now," Peralta said. "They don't want to give P.C. to law enforcement." Probable cause.

We were no longer law enforcement, but in minutes we were out of the truck, waiting to cross the scanty traffic on Central. On Peralta's orders, Robin waited in the locked cab.

"You ought to join me as a P.I."

"No. Why would I want to spend every day with you out in that shack on Grand Avenue?"

"What else are you going to do? I sent you that lawyer, Judson Lee. His case seemed right up your alley. Robin could work with us, too. I've already got more cases than I can handle."

"No. And why did you do that? You're not my boss anymore. We'll sell the house and move to Washington."

"She'll be back."

"Says you, the master of successful marriage."

"You lost one, too, Mapstone, so don't be smug. Not that Sharon didn't warn you about Patty."

That was true enough. I felt the need to defend myself, but there wasn't time. We started across the street and my gut constricted.

"Trust me," he said. "I'm the ideal man to give you advice."

"It's never stopped you."

Then we were on the curb, crossing the sidewalk.

"Well, well, well, the motherfucking former sheriff and his history bitch." This came from a slender man. Beneath his hoodie, he looked somewhere south of thirty, with skin the color of almonds. I had never met him, but people still knew me from television and newspaper appearances that Peralta would orchestrate when we broke an old case.

"Peralta, you the only motherfucker in the La-Ti-No community that's got a nigger pass. Does your *gabacho* here have a nigger pass?"

The three other men, all large and heavily tattooed, watched us silently with the dead, sociopath eyes that had become all too common. My sensibilities stung from hearing the slur, even though it was common on the street.

"He's got a nigger pass from way back." Peralta actually drawled this. "The question is whether it's worth anything down here anymore."

"Here's my black ass," the man said, "there's your Mexican lips. Act accordingly. Bloods have owned this corner since my granddad was banging."

"Whatever you say. Now go shut off that diarrhea coming out of your speakers or I'll put a bullet in your high-end sound system."

The men around the lighter-skinned guy started getting twitchy, but he ordered one of them to turn off the music.

"We need to talk," Peralta said, swinging a leg over the picnic table and pilfering one of the leader's fries. "Don't mind if I do. Mapstone, this here's Andrew "Cut Me Some" Slack, the middle part being his gangster name."

"Hey, fuck you, Peralta. My street name's 'Scandalous.' You know that."

"Sure." Peralta chuckled and ate another of Scandalous' French fries. "I gave him his real nickname because when we first arrested him, he kept saying 'please, cut me some slack.' Anyway, what kind of black name is Andrew?"

Slack ate part of a fish filet and smiled. "Same old racist bastard, yo. But not enough of one to get re-elected. The times they are a-changing."

I kept standing, ready to give Peralta backup if things went bad, but he seemed perfectly comfortable. Every few minutes, I looked back toward Robin. The truck sat unmolested.

Peralta leaned forward on his elbows. "So since we're talking about nicknames and all, what about El Verdugo?"

The backup crew stopped eating and eyed us carefully. Slack chewed intensely and slurped from a giant soft drink.

"Ain't no such," he said. "El Verdugo's an urban legend. And if he ain't, he's down in ole Me-he-ko…" His voice didn't have the same bravado.

"Oh, no," Peralta said. "He's up here. I almost wondered if he was coming after your ass, but then I guess he figured Andrew Slack was the name of some plastic surgeon in Scottsdale…"

"What the fuck you saying?" Slack's voice rose. "El Verdugo? Here? In Phoenix?"

"No, at Disneyland, genius."

Slack was silent. He desperately wanted to look around him, see who might be lurking, but he wouldn't let himself. El Verdugo had a reputation.

He pushed away the tray of food and Peralta helped himself to more fries. "Nobody's been killed down here we don't know who did the killing," Slack said.

When he went sullen, Peralta prompted. "But…"

"Look man, we used to own this area."

"Competition sucks," Peralta said. "The creative destruction of the underground economy."

Peralta, the anti-intellectual, channeling the ghost of Joseph Schumpeter. Now that was new.

"All these fucking 'Cans coming across the border. Bring their gangs with 'em. Keep having babies. What the fuck part of illegal alien don't they understand? The pie's only so big. Only so many white motherfuckers with money to buy drugs. 'Specially now. Bloods are American fucking citizens."

"What about guns?"

Slack hesitated slightly. "You're not even a fucking cop. Why am I talking to you?"

Peralta picked his teeth. "Because you're afraid of El Verdugo. To him you're just another *mayate*."

"Fuck no!" He rose halfway up, puffed out his chest, showed the silver-plated pistol in his waistband, and sat back, all conventions satisfied.

He went on in a conversational voice.

"Word on the street is La Familia is moving in from Southern California. They're taking over some of the foreclosed places out on the west side, using them as safe houses and moving guns for the Gulf Cartel."

"Now why would the cartel want a bunch of bangers when they can just buy from Anglos with clean records making a trip south now and then?" Peralta almost echoed Amy Preston's words.

"It's volume, my man," Stack said. "Word is, La Fam has a smuggling route where they can get truckloads of guns across into Mexico."

"Don't fuck with me," Peralta said. "Smuggling route, my ass."

Slack was undeterred. "Word is, they go across the Indian rez. They've got some Border Patrol on the payroll. Some say they're working directly with the Mexican cops."

"What's your piece of the action?" Peralta asked.

"Wish I had some, el sheriff." He spat toward the sidewalk. "For us, it's all about maintain. We just fighting to keep the business we got."

"Just a hard-working businessman, huh?"

He nodded. "Exact."

Peralta stood. "Thanks. You stay safe now." He nodded to me and we walked back across Central.

Behind us came, "Hey, what are you going to do for me, Peralta? What about El Verdugo? Cut me some slack!"

"See," Peralta said. "He can't help himself."

"What's a *mayate*?"

"Now, Mapstone, I wouldn't want to make you go all politically correct on me."

◇◇◇

Back home, Robin lit the Peace and Prosperity candle and sat with me in the study. After the day of visits to the most scenic parts of the city, I still didn't know where Peralta was going. It felt as if we were up against an army of ghosts and impossible odds.

"Was I just a fool?" Robin asked, her face in her hands. "I always thought, the way I grew up, I had a pretty good bastard detector. But not with Jax. Pedro Alejandro Vega. El Verdugo. What a moron…"

I reached over and touched her shoulder.

She stood, stepped in front of me, and bent down. I felt her long fingers against the sides of my face and then her lips on mine. I kissed her back with minimal stabs of guilt, grasping her waist to pull her closer. Her hair spilled around me and our tongues found each other. It wasn't the best kiss I'd ever had, but it was close, damned close, and if only for a moment it vanquished all the fear and grief and hurt. When I said I didn't trust Robin, it was about this. I didn't trust myself.

"Take me out in the back yard and let's look at the stars," she said.

Our back yard was indeed a good place for stargazing, despite being in the heart of the city. Fourteen-percent humidity would do that. I told her it was too dangerous.

She sighed and sat back on her haunches in front of me. "David, are we ever going to have sex?" She held both my hands. "I don't know about you, but I really need sex."

"Robin, I love Lindsey. I made a vow."

"Love is complicated," she said. "Anyway, she released you from it."

I looked away.

"I know what she said to you in Washington. I know it word for word."

I met her gray eyes. "How can you know that? Lindsey and I were alone, walking on the mall."

"Because she told me."

Chapter Fifteen

Contingency is the great trickster of history. Abraham Lincoln might have given in to the South and let the warring sister go in peace, but he refused. In the desperate months between the election and inauguration of Franklin Roosevelt, when the country faced depression and potentially revolution, a gunman fired at the president-elect. He missed. Housing prices were supposed to go on rising indefinitely, justifying all manner of risk and financial mischief, especially in Phoenix. Only they didn't. And after a long, long dry spell, last May—the causes were the prosaic ones that settle into marriages, even when love and affection persist, and I was as much to blame as she… After that long drought, Lindsey and I had made frenzied love with the air conditioning washing over our bodies. She didn't take time to put in her diaphragm but she thought it would be safe.

When she told me she was pregnant, I withheld my reaction.

"Are you struck dumb?" she asked. "You're the talker in the family, the passionate man whose opinions get him in trouble."

That was true enough, especially in this situation. Yes, the news was so comprehensively staggering that I was struck dumb. But I also knew that Lindsey didn't want children, probably especially not since she had turned forty that year.

But as her dazzling blue eyes grew wet, I just said it. "I'm so happy!" And we embraced tightly, for a long time, laughing until we cried, hugging like silly kids at an eighth-grade dance, our pelvises eight inches apart as if any pressure would somehow damage the life that was growing inside my wife's womb.

"I am too," she said, sobbing and kissing me all over my face. "I didn't know, Dave. I didn't know if I could handle it, a child…" Her voice skipped between weeping. "But, God, I want this child. I want this child with you. You, my true love. My true north."

Now it was my turn to cry, from deep down inside chambers of my emotions and history that I didn't even know existed.

"I want to quit and stay home, be a real mom," Lindsey said. "Will you think less of me? Think I'm Donna Reed?"

"I had a thing for Donna Reed."

"Bap, bap, bap." She shadowboxed my face.

Of course, it was all right. Lindsey had always loved the house and the garden more than her job at the Sheriff's Office, talented as she was. The house was paid off. We had some savings. I would still be employed by Peralta. We would make it work.

I wanted to make martinis to celebrate, but of course that was out, at least for Lindsey. As she joked and danced around me in the kitchen, I made one for me, and put shaken cold water in a glass for her.

It was the beginning of the three happiest months of my life.

Peralta called the next night. He said to be ready to go out at ten.

"Go where."

"To meet La Familia. Did you think I was just taking you on a free tour of gangland yesterday? Arrangements had to be made."

I let the phone sit silently by my ear, bad feelings coursing through me despite the merry blue Peace and Prosperity candle sitting on the desk.

He said, "Make sure Robin wears her vest. And bring your friend, Mister Five-Seven. Bring the Colt Python, too."

"Maybe we can let Robin stay at your house," I said.

"No. She has to come. That's part of the deal."

"What deal?" I demanded.

But he had already hung up.

◇◇◇

The *norteño* music came blaring out of the open door of the Los Arcos Night Club. Guitar, accordion, bass, and drums, accompanying a tenor's fervent croon. Inside, however, the musicians were only on a sound system and business was slow. Two men in pressed jeans, neat cowboy shirts, and immaculate Stetsons sat at the bar and watched the two Anglos come in accompanying the former sheriff. Their expressions weren't hostile; more of curiosity. At the end of the bar, Bill was smoking and drinking a Budweiser.

"That's illegal." Peralta indicated the cigarette, now banned in a bar or restaurant.

"So arrest me." Bill gave a wide smile. A bartender came over and I ordered two Negra Modelos for Robin and me. Peralta wanted a Bud.

"Who is that?" Robin pointed to a ten-inch-tall porcelain statue behind the bar. It depicted a man with emphatic thick eyebrows and a black mustache, dressed in a white shirt and black scarf. A small devotional candle was burning beside it.

"Jesus Malverde," Bill said. "He was the angel of the poor."

"The narco saint of Sinaloa," Peralta said.

"Don't be disrespectful." Bill looked at the statue and crossed himself. "He was like Robin Hood, only more. I seek his intercession." He looked morose. "Magdalena says he's from the devil, she won't have his statue in the shop."

My Robin, no hood, tried to change the subject. "Tell me about this music."

"It's Chalino. Chalino Sanchez. He was the greatest *corrido* singer. Balladeer."

"He was a play outlaw," Peralta said. "Real ones ambushed and killed him in Sinaloa."

"So cynical," Bill said. "You can't understand this world without understanding the *narcocorridos*."

"Is that what he's singing about now?" Robin asked. "About the traffickers?"

"No. This is a love song. But it's lost love and bitterness. He sings that he keeps the bitterness to himself. It's the *corridos pesados* that are about the heavy things, drug smuggling and murder, exploitation and the poor fighting back any way they can. But it's life, right? These are very moral songs, when you think about it."

Peralta swigged the last of his beer. "Let's get the details, Bill. I'm not here for the local color."

They bent their heads close together and spoke quickly in Spanish, too fast and too low for me to understand.

The wide, dark avenues took us farther west. Wide, dark avenues ran through my soul. The pickup's cab felt stifling even though the heat was off and the vent was running on low. Peralta said Bill had arranged for us to meet with the Phoenix boss of La Familia. The catch: we had to bring Robin. I didn't like it.

"Do you want to live in fear for the rest of your life?" he asked.

Robin spoke quickly. "No."

"Wait a damn minute," I said, but Peralta sped on, making every green light. "Robin, I don't think you should do this."

She said, "I have to."

We were just about out of Maryvale when Peralta spun the wheel and we entered the large parking lot of a shuttered big-box store. Phoenix had maybe one million square feet of empty big boxes, crushed by the recession or left behind when a retailer moved to a newer mega-store out in newer suburbia. This looked as if it had once been a Home Depot. The building was dark. The streetlights were off. The parking lot was empty. He shifted into park on the far edge of the lot and drummed his fingers on the steering wheel. Robin put her hand in mine.

The clock read 11:11 when two pairs of headlights came in from the west. The vehicles parked directly opposite us across the block of empty asphalt. Peralta clicked his high beams twice. In a second, one of the vehicles shot back two flashes.

"We're going to walk to the middle of the lot," Peralta said. "So are they."

"Why?" My back was suddenly aching.

"Because. They'll know we don't have PD backup. And we'll know they don't have a shooter hidden in the back seat of one of those cars."

"This doesn't guarantee any of that," I said. "They could drive up and kill us. This is crazy."

"Maybe," Peralta said. "It's the rules of engagement they demanded, or no meeting. We meet on open ground so everybody can see what's around them."

Peralta swiveled to face Robin. "You don't have to go through with this."

I said, "I don't want her to do it. This is too dangerous."

She sighed heavily and squeezed my hand. "Let's do it."

Four figures were already walking into the lot. The car headlights remained on. Peralta left the truck idling, our lights on, too. They barely cut through the gloom of the vast space. I opened the door and swung myself out, eager to find firm ground. I unzipped my jacket.

We walked at an easy pace toward the silhouettes. I made Robin walk behind me, and I moved in step with Peralta, a pitiful skirmish line. Robin had a different analogy.

"It's like the old West," she said softly.

"If anything goes wrong, you run back and drive away," I said over my shoulder. "I mean it."

I forced down the dread inside and felt the calm that extreme situations always gave me. I didn't understand it. Panic attacks when I was in the quiet shelter of scholarship. Clarity and focus in an emergency. "Frosty," as Peralta, the Vietnam vet, said approvingly. It seemed to go against something I had heard years ago, attributed to Confucius: about three methods to gaining wisdom. "The first is reflection, which is the highest. The second is imitation, which is the easiest. The third is experience, which is the bitterest." Maybe it's why I didn't feel wise. I didn't even know if Confucius had actually said it.

Peralta slow-walked so the four men arrived at the center of the lot first. He was plotting one of those tactical solutions, maybe several.

"Well, well, well, the former sheriff of Maricopa County."

The speaker was a man of medium height, wearing a zippered cotton warm-up top with horizontal stripes and a stylized L on the breast pocket. He had large, dark eyes, a stubble goatee, and mustache setting off a wide mouth. Beneath a red ball cap, he looked as if he could go from zero to thug in under six seconds. On his chest was a gold cross with Christ crucified upon it, gleaming in the strange light. Except for the cross, everything was in the half-shadow of the contending headlights. His buddies reminded me of the Hispanic bangers I had watched that hot day last summer, as we waited for the gasoline to flow. They were lean and muscled, wore jeans and sleeveless white shirts to show off their tattoos. The three silent ones carried compact automatic weapons and they were aiming them at us.

"And who are you?" Peralta's voice was familiar and comforting.

"Mero Mero."

"Good. I wouldn't want to deal with *el pequeño*." A little one.

"We'll have your guns," Mero Mero said.

"That doesn't seem sporting." Peralta's tone was unchanged but he subtly shifted his posture.

"Too bad. Rules is rules."

We all stood and watched each other for what seemed like several eras. I didn't know everything about Peralta's moods and moves, but here I was certain.

"Okay," Peralta said, affecting his peculiar insouciance. "No problem."

Now I was afraid.

Peralta pulled out his Sig Sauer P220 Combat semi-automatic, chambered for .45 caliber. He held it by the barrel, an offering.

"Go ahead, Mapstone. Take out your guns."

I looked at him.

"Do it," he ordered.

One of the bangers laughed. "This *bolillo's* so scared he has two." He tilted down his gun and spat heavily on the ground. And they all laughed. Part of my mind wondered where he had picked up the old Chicano slang for white boy, not meant in a favorable sense.

The frivolity provided the nanoseconds for Peralta to drop the .45 back into shooting position and have it aimed at Mero Mero's head. The bullet only had to travel two feet.

By that time I had the Python in my left hand and the Five-Seven in my right. I had trained for years on left-handed shooting. Peralta demanded it, in case a deputy was shot or injured in the hand he favored. I clicked off the safety of the Five-Seven, aimed at two of the other men. The spitter looked at me with wide eyes.

I said, *"Si levantas esa arma, te mato."* If you raise that weapon, I'll kill you. Or that's what I hoped I said: the gun stayed down.

"I guess this is what they call a Mexican standoff," Peralta said. "But it's not really, because I can kill all of you before my partner here even has to exercise his trigger fingers."

Seconds turned into minutes. Spitter didn't raise his gun. Every now and then the whoosh of an oblivious motorist cut into the silence.

Mero Mero said, "It's cool. *Es chida.*" And his minions relaxed their arms.

I breathed sweet, dusty air.

Peralta lowered the .45, kept it out, and I did the same with my two life-preservers.

"Is this the girl?" Mero Mero said.

Peralta nodded.

"Let me look at you, *chica.*"

Robin stepped from behind me and the top dog evaluated her with a lascivious smile.

"I don't know you, *chica.* I might like to."

"Quit fucking around," Peralta said.

"Let me tell you something, ex-lawman. I only come out here because my uncle owes a favor to Guillermo. I don't owe you shit." He pulled off his cap and scratched his short hair. "But, what the fuck, I don't know this girl. Don't know anything about her. Don't have anything against her. Should I?"

"No," Peralta said. He holstered his weapon. I knew it was a gesture, and I kept mine ready to rock although down at my sides. He said, "I know you're not a gangster like the *mayates*," he said. "You're a warrior." One of the men ran his hand across an elaborate tattoo on his upper arm. I could make out a feathered helmet and a profile.

Peralta went on, "I'm a warrior, too. Maybe different sides, but a warrior. My Aztec blood is as pure as yours."

"What are you saying?"

"Warrior-to-warrior, your boys sent her a severed head. That's disrespectful. She's a civilian. She's not a part of our war."

"What the fuck?" Genuine surprise melted his gang face. "We didn't…"

I said, "You didn't send her a severed head? Why did you have one of your homeboys watching my house?" I even gave him the address.

He blinked hard and shook his head. "I don't even know you."

Peralta honed in. "Am I talking to Mero Mero or not?"

The gang face returned, full of something to prove.

"I hope so," Peralta said.

"I speak with authority," the man said with great formality. "I don't know either of these *gabachos*. Warrior-to-warrior, La Familia has nothing…"

His next word was lost in the bright red fog that suddenly came out of his head. The gold cross around his neck shimmered brightly.

Then we heard the explosion.

I didn't think or hesitate. I just tackled Robin, drove her to the pavement, and lay on top of her, even before Peralta yelled, "Down!"

From the surface of the parking lot, I watched Mero Mero's crew enjoy a last moment of confusion, not knowing whether to rush to their fallen leader, open fire on us, or heed Peralta's commands. They did none of these, and each one succumbed to head shots. One, two, three…gone. That fast. Each shot involved a deep, artillery-like concussion and echo.

I stayed on top of Robin and she didn't move. My heart was about to jerk free of my chest and run across the parking lot. The headlights from the vehicles now seemed like an especially bad idea. Peralta's truck seemed a football field away.

"That's a .50-cal sniper rifle," Peralta said, crouched and searching with the barrel of his sidearm. "He's got a flash suppressor. Maybe he's on the roof."

Then the shots stopped.

Peralta didn't wait long. "Back to the truck," he ordered, in the voice of the Army Ranger that he once was. I ran with my hands on Robin, shielding her. My back felt gigantic and vulnerable. We reached the truck in seconds, propelled by gallons of adrenaline, and climbed inside.

After making sure Robin was no more than bruised from me pushing her down, I pulled out my cell.

"What are you doing?" Peralta took it from my hand.

"Calling 911. What else should we do?"

We had always been the law. Our obligation, once the civilian was secure, was to pursue the shooter. Peralta just looked at me as if it was a stupid question.

"We get the fuck out of here."

He dropped the truck into gear and roared out, turned west, and picked up the 101 beltway that would take us back to the center city.

Chapter Sixteen

"They had a chance to kill all of us and they didn't." I spoke into the dark, cigar-perfumed cab of Peralta's truck. The speedometer needle rested on a lawful sixty-five and we pirouetted through an interchange and went east again on the wide freeway.

"We were exposed all that time. How many minutes? The shooter could have taken all of us out. He could have shot Robin. Why were we spared?"

"I need you to be quiet now, Mapstone."

And that was all Peralta said. His face was set except for the subtle tension in his jaw. I put my arm around Robin to ease her trembling, then I fully embraced her the rest of the way into the city. Peralta glanced at us, then focused ahead, and kept his own counsel. The sound of the rifle still sounded in my head.

We came off the Papago Freeway at Seventh Avenue, just before it entered the tunnel under the deck park. The light was green and I got only a quick glance at my old grade school, built in the 1920s with grand columns and palm trees out front, the alma mater of Barry Goldwater. And me. How did I get into this life, where I was competent at several things but brilliant at none? How many bad choices had I made since I was a student there, terrified by the duck-and-cover-drills, learning to fight against the school bullies, and impatiently watching the clock. At that age you don't realize how quickly the clock runs out. Robin gently pulled away and sat up.

"What happened back there?" she asked, her voice wavering.

"I don't know," Peralta said.

"Where are we going?"

"To find Antonio."

This made my passive-aggressive side, never one of my prime movers, shift into aggressive-aggressive. "No, fuck no. You pull over and give us some answers, or we're out of this."

To my astonishment, he complied.

He reached into the glove box and removed a portable police radio, switching channels until he found the one he wanted. Civilians couldn't get this at Radio Shack, since so many police bands were encrypted now to prevent criminals from monitoring calls—and many routine ones were transmitted to cruiser laptops, anyway. It didn't surprise me that Peralta had one. The radio was busy with units responding to the shooting on the west side. On the sidewalk, a man shambled north with his belongings in two large, black plastic bags.

Peralta pulled a seven-inch cigar out of his jacket pocket, clipped it, and struck a match to light the end in a circle, ensuring it would burn evenly. The electric motor of the window whirred and he puffed out into the cool, dry air.

"Bill's been clean for years," he said. "But from time-to-time, he's been a valuable go-between for me. He has friends and relatives in the life. Because he did his time and never gave up his friends, he has respect. I've worked to never put him at risk, never make him seem like he's a *snoflon*, a snitch. So that meant I had to give something up sometimes to get something better. Understand?"

I wasn't sure I wanted to understand. Peralta's wings spread far beyond my little cold-case boutique. I said, "So that was the deal tonight? Meet with La Fam and make a deal to save Robin?"

He took another puff and nodded.

"What did you have to give in return?"

"All sorts of things."

I let that alone. But I asked how he even knew if these now-dead bangers could speak for La Fam.

"Mero Mero? His real name is Carlos Mendoza. He's one of the top dogs of La Fam in the United States. Check out his sheet. The gold medals start with homicide and go from there. This is not just another street gang in Phoenix."

"And he said he spoke with authority," Robin said, hope in her voice. "He didn't know me. He said he didn't have anything against me."

"That's what he said." Peralta studied the bright orange tip of the cigar. Cars zipped by benignly on Seventh Avenue.

Now Mero Mero and his crew were dead, taken out as accurately as bad guys in the sights of Marine scout snipers in Iraq. I asked what that meant.

"Maybe the theory has been wrong."

"Are you ever going to clue us in on this theory?" I tried to keep my anger down, without much success. "I love theories."

He said nothing, so I just let loose all the stress of the evening. "You've known more about this than you've been telling me since the start. You just show up at the house where El Verdugo was tortured and beheaded. You load me up on ordnance at home, stuff you just happen to have in the trunk. Then Kate Vare drops a case that just happens to lead to a gun shop being watched by ATF. And here's my good friend the sheriff, taking me to meet his old gang buddy and some Mexican cop. Now a top La Fam guy is taken out and we get to walk away. What the hell is going on?"

"You need to calm down." He gently tapped an inch of ash off into the air. "I'm on retainer to the state Attorney General. That happened after I left office so we could continue an operation that's been going on for a year."

"The gun-runners."

"Exactly. The A.G. doesn't have much confidence in the new sheriff. I have the institutional knowledge. So there I was."

"You made Kate Vare back off?"

"It didn't take much," he said. "You ever read the Bad Phoenix Cops blog? The guy that writes it has great sources inside the department. There's lots of turmoil in command and the homicide bureau right now. And it turns out Vare is being investigated by PSB…" The Professional Standards Bureau, what was once called Internal Affairs. "Botched case management on the Baseline killer. Alleged. The families are suing the city. Maybe it's political—it's a very screwed-up department. But she began leaving you alone right when PSB came down on her. Not a coincidence, if you ask me. Vare had a hard-on for you, but Robin's an investigative dead end. The new detective team would go after this from the El Verdugo and gang angle. At some point, the A.G. told them about our interest. So it doesn't surprise me they've left you alone."

"And what exactly is your interest?"

"We know there's been a big uptick in weapons crossing the border from Arizona gun dealers. There are a few, like the Jesus Is Lord Pawn Shop, that sell in volume."

"The Blood leader said La Fam has a new route to move guns for the Gulf cartel."

"That confirms other intel we've had," he said. "The feds and the Mexican authorities took down the top Gulf boss a year ago, extradited him to Houston, and he's been cooperating. So plenty of the Gulf cartel's reliable U.S. gun suppliers in Texas have been prosecuted. They're under real pressure now from the Mexican army, so they really need a new supply chain."

"They sound like multinational corporations," Robin said, "only with guns."

"In lots of ways they are," Peralta said. "The cartels have billions of dollars at their disposal. 'Cartel' isn't even an accurate word anymore. These are highly organized entities. They can employ top-notch accountants to help launder the money. They compete for market share to sell drugs and tax the *coyotes* that bring the illegals across the border to work in legitimate industries. They work with gangs in this country. Consider those the subcontractors. Sometimes they cooperate with each other, because bloodshed is bad for business. Sometimes they don't."

"So what was the theory?" I prodded.

He waved his flaming cigar wand. "That the Sinaloa cartel found out that the Gulf cartel was poaching in a supply chain it considers its own, namely the perfectly legal industry of Arizona gun sales."

"And they sent in a trouble-shooter, El Verdugo…"

He nodded. "To do a strategic hit on a high-value target, maybe a major gun dealer. Send the message: Don't do business with the Gulf boys." He nursed the stogie. The tobacco was such high-quality it must have been Cuban. "Mind you, I was skeptical when you found the snake's-head ring. Nobody really knows who El Verdugo is, much less that he'd be up here. Antonio is convinced, the guy Robin was seeing was Vega."

"But La Fam, doing the Gulf cartel's dirty work, got him first."

"That was the theory."

I asked why Robin's involvement hadn't derailed the theory.

He shook his head. "She's an attractive woman, clean record, middle-class, artsy. She might have been useful to El Verdugo's cover. Hell, Mapstone, you might have been useful to his cover. He was in Phoenix pretending to be a professor and fooling both of you. It let him fit right in."

"So it was tonight. Somebody took out La Fam, who was supposed to have taken out El Verdugo. Only maybe they didn't even do that, or send the head to Robin. And you don't know who fired those shots tonight."

He took the cigar out of his mouth, started to say something, and just nodded.

"Maybe Robin is in the clear." He spoke slowly. "You haven't had any other trouble since you took down the guy in the pickup. Tonight La Fam said they didn't even know her. And whoever was doing the shooting could have killed us all and didn't."

"Unless they want to snatch her alive."

"Why not do it tonight, then?" he said. "We were totally exposed. This shooter was good enough to take both me and Mapstone out and leave you alive, Robin. He didn't."

I sighed. "Why don't I feel better? Somebody delivered that package to her for a reason."

He tossed away the cigar. "Maybe it was a demonstration. Nothing more than that."

I asked what he meant.

"To show their power. They can find El Verdugo in this very respectable cover he's taken on. They can kill him. And deliver his head to his girlfriend in a very public demonstration of their power. And don't forget you live there, too. A deputy sheriff, and one who was in the media with his old cases. They showed, 'We can do this.' And maybe it was nothing more than that."

"I never picked you for the cockeyed optimist."

"That may not be our biggest problem. Whoever killed those four La Fam guys wasn't some banger. You see where this is heading? It's only been a matter of time. Maybe this is it."

Robin said, "The war going on down in Mexico is here now."

The truck rumbled to life. "That's why I want to talk to Antonio."

I asked about us.

"Go home. Have a drink for me. Have two."

Chapter Seventeen

Peralta had already driven away when I saw the FedEx package leaning neatly against the front door. It was letter-sized. Too small to contain a head; eyeballs or ears, maybe. Anthrax or a small explosive, definitely. I asked Robin if she was expecting anything—neither was I. On the long walk up to the door, I thought about calling the police. I scanned the dark sidewalks, seeing nothing, not even a car parked on the street. But I was so damned tired, had seen so much death that night, that I just picked it up and unlocked the door.

Once the alarm was disarmed, I took the envelope into the study and zipped it open, keeping the opening away from my face. Inside were some Xerox copies of old newspaper clippings and a five-thousand-dollar check drawn on the account of Judson Lee, Attorney at Law. It wasn't signed. He had included a note: "My offer still stands."

"He wants you pretty bad," Robin said.

"But I don't want him."

"It might do you some good. Get outside yourself for a while. I know you can use the money."

"Peralta wants to rope me into being a P.I."

"A private dick, huh?" Her eyes gleamed merrily. She undid her bun and shook out her hair across her shoulders. It gleamed with colors ranging from light brown to gold. "I'll help you. I'm a good researcher—a curator has to have those skills. This would be a healthy break from trying to keep track of all these cartels and gangs. It can be the return of the History Shamus."

That had been Lindsey's nickname for me, but I didn't mind that Robin used it. It actually felt good. My eye wandered to the photo on the desk. It showed me, Lindsey and Robin last summer in Flagstaff. The weather was gentle in the high country and our smiles genuine and joyous. Robin was the only other person who knew that Lindsey was pregnant, and this drew them even closer together. We decided we would wait until Lindsey passed the three-month mark to tell anyone else.

Our new reality was only beginning to settle in. Much of our conversations revolved around the kind of parents we wouldn't be. We wouldn't call our child a kid, which is a goat. We wouldn't take a newborn into the Sheriff's Office and parade it around like some consumer product bought at Walmart. Our child would be raised in a real neighborhood with front porches and neighbors who knew each other, in a house with books, music, and ideas, a doting aunt who would teach her about art, and most of all, a house of love. She would go to a public school, just as we had done. I called the baby a she, and Lindsey was convinced it would be a son. We laughed over it and agreed to let God surprise us.

Robin picked up the photo, studied it, and replaced it on the desk. She sat on the blotter and looked down at me.

"When we were growing up, there was such…chaos." Robin searched for that last word. "Linda had Lindsey Faith when she was sixteen. So you can imagine the sexual competition between the two, when Lindsey was sixteen and luminous, and Linda was an attractive woman in her early thirties." She smiled. "I paid good money to therapists to learn all this shit. Lindsey Faith was the peacemaker, my protector. She kept the family together through it all."

"Why do you call her Lindsey Faith?"

"Because it's a beautiful name."

"What's your middle name?"

"Someday I'll tell you."

"You were the teenage rebel," I said.

"How'd you guess? We moved every couple of years. There was always a new boyfriend and most of them were creeps who wanted to sleep with Lindsey or me. Seriously. This was what we grew up in. Our mom wasn't a bad person. She was just very creative and very overwhelmed by life. She wanted to be an artist and she ended up working as a cocktail waitress."

"Lindsey said she had schizophrenia. That's why she had always said she didn't want children. And it was all right with me."

Robin tilted her head, closed her eyes, summoning a past both sisters would rather forget. "My bet is Linda was bipolar and it was aggravated by drugs and anger and heartbreak in her life, but what do I know?"

"And Lindsey lived her life to not become her mother."

"Yes. And I think it was a struggle for her. Mother and daughter were very alike when I think back on it. I was the foundling. She fought to be normal and stable. She had her devils, always hearing Linda's voice in her head, that she wasn't good enough, that she was a screw-up. I used to joke with her and say, 'Turn off your Linda Unit'—that critical voice she heard in her head. She never did. She just kept those devils chained up."

"Don't we all?"

"I suppose. Every family has its skeletons. Ours was a skeleton festival." She said it without humor. "I don't know how we survived."

I said, "Lindsey blames me for what happened."

She rubbed her hands gently on her jeans. "That's not true, David. You blame yourself. She blames herself. She wanted so much to give you a child, so your DNA could carry on in the world."

"And hers."

After a long silence, Robin said, "I remember after we first met, we went out one night. I think I put the moves on you. Tall, smart men always get me going."

"Sexual competition again?"

"Oh, I'm a free spirit, David. I make no apologies. But I do remember telling you that Lindsey had a baby when she was in high school."

I did remember, all of it.

"You just thought I was messing with you. But it's the truth. She got pregnant. The father was one of the high-school hoods, but she had a crush on him, and was so naive. And she got pregnant. Now I think it was a cry for help, as they say. Anyway, Linda wouldn't let her keep the baby. She put it up for adoption. Lindsey Faith never got over that. So in her mind, she's lost two babies."

I fought the tightness in my throat.

"It's been an awful night," Robin said. "I've never seen anyone killed before. I was so afraid for you. Let's go to bed."

I looked at the photo again.

"I can't call her to say we're okay, can I?"

"No," Robin said.

"Because she won't talk to me, or because she's not even at her apartment?" *She's not wearing her wedding band.*

Robin gave me a look, her eyes sleepy and her mouth in something like a half-smile. Then she looked away. "David, you've given me a great gift. You've brought out a gentle side I never knew I had. You've watched out for me. With all that happened tonight, I felt safe and taken care of. When you covered me with your body, you were willing to die in order to save me." She reached down and mussed my hair. "It's so much more than that. You've let me into you. I would never betray that trust."

Now it was my turn to look away. I felt so sad and strange. And so suddenly aware of how dependent I had become on protecting Robin, on being the knight in, well, tarnished armor, and, yes, I had let her in. Dr. Sharon wouldn't approve.

Robin hadn't given me a straight answer about Lindsey. But, of course, she had.

Chapter Eighteen

I started on the case the next day. Case? No, a research project.
I was not a deputy any longer, not a private investigator. I was
just a guy at loose ends.

We had a long lunch with Judson Lee at the Phoenician,
poolside at the Oasis Bar & Grill. The dismal economy seemed
far away, but like nearby Scottsdale, the resort had a dull falseness
to it. Miami depended on tourists, too. But it was sexy, edgy,
and authentic. Phoenix just had a lot of people, and in the places
where most people lived, no soul. Nobody would ever do "CSI
Phoenix" for television.

The server, an attractive brunette in her twenties, seemed
to know him well and he flirted relentlessly with her. The posh
surroundings were a shock when compared with our recent
sojourns. The clientele were all white, all rich. Add in all the
people in Maricopa County who were white, poor, and desperately looking for someone, anyone, to blame for their straits—a
substantial demographic—and this was the constituency of the
new sheriff. I tried to set the thought aside.

Lee asked what I knew about Harley Talbott. I asked him how
many hours he had. But after his smile faded I went through
the basics. The multi-millionaire had died in 1990. He bridged
the eras between old and new Phoenix, coming out of a pioneer
Arizona family, building the city's largest liquor distributor-
ship, owning land, cattle, and a cotton-seed company. The

rumors about Talbott's connections to organized crime went back decades. His liquor business—and alleged bookmaking operation—was said to have had its start in Talbott's friendship with the remnants of the Al Capone mob. He owned senators, congressmen, and judges, thanks to his political contributions.

"How much of this is true?" Lee wanted to know. "I'm from Chicago, so I can tell you about Al Capone. Phoenix, there's history I don't know."

"I suspect a lot of it was true," I said. "This was a wide-open town back in the old days. As the city grew, the line between the establishment and the mob was very porous. There are old rumors about Del Webb, the man who built Sun City. The same is even true with Barry Goldwater. It was a mobbed up town, and everybody touched it one way or the other. But you'll still find Talbott defenders even today."

"I don't want his defenders," Lee said. "As you can understand, my loyalty is to my client, and I help solve problems."

"And Mr. DeSimone's problem is the prison stretch his grandfather did back in the 1940s?"

"Yes. As you saw from the newspaper clippings, a liquor store was firebombed. It was a store that wouldn't play by Harley Talbott's rules. Paolo DeSimone was arrested, tried, convicted, and imprisoned. It's true Paolo worked as a driver for Talbott. But he always maintained his innocence. My client wants to know if that's true. If it is, we have the resources to try to clear his name."

"If he did it for Talbott, it doesn't make sense that Talbott couldn't get him off," I said. "He pretty much owned the cops and the courts."

Robin asked what became of Paolo.

"That's the tragedy. He got out of prison and lived just three more years. Cancer. He died broken, almost penniless, his family destitute. Harley Talbott lived to be ninety-two."

"How awful." When Robin said it, Lee reached out his old leather hand and tapped her comfortingly.

My heart was not in this. That morning's *Republic* had the west-side killings inside the Valley & State section. "Four men

found shot in parking lot." The editors just couldn't bring themselves to bump the latest health news or feel-good story about
100 jobs at a solar-panel factory off page one. They probably all
lived in Ahwatukee or Chandler and had no idea of what was
really happening in the city. If a white person had been killed in
Scottsdale, it would have been Page One news. Why did I care
about this case? But watching Lee's friendly, imploring face, I
agreed to take it on. I warned him that I might not be able to
find any new evidence, with virtually every player in the case
dead by now, and the condition of records uncertain. I also said
the facts would speak for themselves.

"It might be that Paolo was guilty. Families have secrets, and
Nick might find out things he really doesn't want to know."

"If that's the case, so be it." He said it without pause and went
back to telling the server what pretty eyes she had. She rubbed
his tanned, bald head and he smiled and flicked out his tongue
like a contented lizard.

"Mr. Lee is such a charmer," she said.

My cell rang as we were getting the car from the resort's valet. It
was Peralta. Come to his office. It wasn't a request.

So I drove out of the surreal green expanse of the Phoenician:
designed, manicured, beloved, flowers and bright green grass under
perfect palm trees. Then through the comfortable old wealth of the
lush Arcadia district, past Biltmore Fashion Park, now hideously
"modernized," west on Camelback Road as the real estate became
seedier and seedier, land not beloved, places not built to be cared
about. Poor people waited in large clusters at bus stops for the
city's evermore diminished transit. The sun beat on them with an
intensity that belied the eighty degrees on the thermometer. In
thirty minutes, we turned on the broad diagonal of Grand Avenue
and then bumped into what passed for Peralta's parking lot.

"It would be really cool if he restored the neon," Robin said,
indicating the Easy 8 Auto Court sign. I studied its odd shape
and realized it had once shown a cowboy throwing a rope.

"I'll let you tell him that."

I held the door for Robin and walked in talking, telling Peralta that I was taking on the work for Judson Lee, even though it was probably a waste of time. Then I noticed Antonio, the Mexican cop, sitting on the other desk, slowly swinging his leg, smoking a thin cigar. He had on the same jeans and blue blazer. Expensive lizard-skin boots had been added to the ensemble. I shut up.

"It's been a productive morning," Peralta said after we were seated. "A joint agency task force raided a house in a gated community in Mesa this morning."

I waited, suddenly pulled out of corrupt 1940s Phoenix. But I couldn't resist. "How many Mormons did you nab?"

"We arrested three men. All Mexican nationals. All heavily armed."

"Did they…Last night?" Robin let it hang.

"It's a good probability. One is a former Mexican Army airborne sniper. Now he's working for the Sinaloa cartel. This was an assassination squad."

"Did you find a rifle?"

"Not yet," Peralta said. "We will."

"So they were avenging La Fam's hit on El Verdugo?" I said. Neither man spoke.

I could see Robin's expression cloud over. She had taken comfort in Mero Mero saying he had nothing against her, didn't know her.

She said, "He wasn't El Verdugo." I gave her points for loyalty.

The room smelled of mildew, no easy thing in Phoenix. It was a smell that mingled with cigar smoke and congregated in my senses as nobody spoke for several minutes. Peralta and Antonio exchanged glances.

Then Antonio said, "That's true."

"What?" Robin sat up straight.

"He wasn't El Verdugo."

"How do you know?" I asked.

"Because I killed El Verdugo in Juarez a year ago."

"Oh, my God." She cupped her face in her hands. "Then, who…"

"Let's get something straight." Peralta's tone was harsh. "What we're about to tell you is off the record. You can never tell anyone." He stared at me.

I struggled to keep my anger in check—all the lies they had casually told us, when Robin's life was at risk. I slowly nodded.

"El Verdugo was alone when I caught up with him," Antonio said. "He drew, I was faster. *Adios, chingaso.* We buried him in Juarez in an unmarked grave, kept the information from the other cops. His buddies never knew, either. So we hijacked his identity."

Antonio gently set the cigar in a large glass ashtray. "We made it seem like he'd disappeared and gone rogue. Every now and again, I'd get to a killing first—an easy thing in my country—and use that snake's-head ring on the victim. Just to keep the stories and rumors coming. Sinaloa went crazy. Their man was killing them. But the Gulf boys had no comfort. El Verdugo was killing them, too. And killing Los Zetas."

"But not really," Robin said. "You were just faking it."

"Precisely," Antonio said. "But it was useful. Sow chaos. This was a very closely held secret, especially among my colleagues, but even with my friends the Americans, who have shown they have a weakness for cartel bribes, too."

"Three months ago," Peralta said, "we picked up intel that a subject in Phoenix was shopping for a hit man. He met with an undercover officer, but wouldn't bite. He wanted the best. He wanted El Verdugo. Asked for him by name."

"Who was this party?" I asked.

Peralta pursed his lips. "Barney. At the Jesus Is Lord Pawn Shop."

I softly said, "Guns, knives, ammunition."

Antonio said, "ATF inserted a deep undercover agent to pose as El Verdugo. He was one of their best. I gave him the snake's head ring. You knew him by his real name, Jax Delgado."

I heard Robin's throat catch. My stomach burned. "You've known this all along? Damn you to hell, Mike."

"The A.G. wouldn't let me tell you." Peralta folded his arms. "And ATF sure as hell wouldn't. Amy Preston went nuts after you showed up at her house asking about the gun shop."

"Why are you telling us now?"

"It just seems right," Peralta said. "With this arrest, I think we're going to be able to close the case. These guys somehow picked up Delgado's trail and killed him. Maybe it was because they thought he was the real Verdugo and this was payback time. Maybe they sniffed out his cover." He noticed my expression. "When they were torturing him, maybe he talked about Robin. Or maybe they followed him and knew where she lived."

"The autopsy on Delgado said he'd been tased," Antonio said. "That may have been how they initially took him down. These guys had a Taser. We're going to show their photos to the staff at the FedEx shop where his head was shipped from." His tone made it sound like so much freight. "See if anybody can pick them out."

I said, "What about last night?"

"Because La Fam is working with the Gulf cartel to move arms," Antonio said, "the Sinaloans also took out Mero Mero and his crew. They probably followed you last night. This hit squad was up here on serious business. My guess is Barney would have been the next patient on the torture table, for doing business with the Gulf cartel and La Fam. Maybe he'd get off easy. Lose a finger or an ear and have to keep supplying Sinaloa."

"Slow down," I said. "Jax made contact with Barney?"

Peralta nodded. "No Arizona jury is going to convict a licensed gun dealer for selling firearms, no matter how many people they kill in Mexico. With Jax, we had Barney on hiring a hit man. We thought we could get more. Evidence that he was selling firearms in bulk to the Gulf cartel. We could shut him down forever."

Robin clasped her arms tightly around her chest. "Does this mean we're safe?"

Both men said "yes" simultaneously.

"They ought to just legalize drugs," Robin whispered. "All this death, and for what?"

Antonio said, "This isn't about drugs anymore. This is about power."

I was drowning in the bucket of information they had just dumped on us. "If he was on the job, why would he tell us his real name?"

Peralta shrugged. "Maybe he met somebody he cared about."

Robin abruptly stood and strode out across the ancient linoleum.

I had many questions, but followed her out. She fell into my arms by the car and sobbed hard, her tears soaking through my shirt while a freight train trundled past, steel slamming upon steel.

Chapter Nineteen

The clippings from the old *Phoenix Gazette* told of how McNamara's Liquors on Van Buren Street burned in the early hours of September 20th, 1940. The fire marshal said it was arson. Within two weeks, police had arrested Paolo DeSimone for what was now being called a "fire bombing." The newspaper displayed a booking photo of a slender, hatchet-faced man with a pencil moustache. It listed him as an "itinerant laborer" and gave his age as twenty-eight. He had signed a confession, and unlike today, the case rapidly moved to trial within a month. DeSimone didn't take the stand. The jury convicted him of arson and he was sentenced to ten years at the State Prison in Florence. That was the end of the news, and if the reporting was halfway accurate, things didn't look good for Paolo.

But we would try.

My large office in the old County Courthouse had been full of police and court records from the 1910s through the 1940s. The county hadn't been much interested in them, and over the years with Peralta I had amassed a wonderful library of old Phoenix crime. It was my anti-Google and had done right by me in dozens of old cases. Except for the boxes I had brought home in Lindsey's car that December day, I had left most of it behind. And a quick check of the files I had showed little of utility. The Phoenix Police logbook showed a notation, written in efficient script, that the east-side squad car had been dispatched to a fire at McNamara's Liquors at 2:21 a.m. on September 20th. It was still a fairly new innovation to have two or three radio-equipped cars out in the city late at night. The population of Phoenix was 65,414. The area within the city limits was maybe twelve miles.

The new cases were online, the old ones stored away in paper files. In theory, at least. I made a call and a friend from the county got me into the deep storage of the Superior Court clerk. *Arizona v. DeSimone* was not there. It felt strange being down at the county office buildings, seeing the line of prisoner buses parked and the corrections officers smoking outside the Madison Street Jail, except the sign had a stranger's name on it as sheriff. I had no desire to have lunch, as I so often once did, at Sing Hi. I didn't want to run into old colleagues from the S.O. or the county attorney's office and have to make explanation, much less get angry over the treatment of Peralta.

It was a relief to be sent over to the State Archives, near the capitol. The building was new but the state's financial troubles had cut the hours to nearly nothing and the crackpots in the Legislature were trying to take its space. Criminal transcripts might eventually make their way here, both for historical value and because the defendant had a right to appeal. In reality, the records were often a mess. This would especially be true for the DeSimone case. It lacked the notoriety of, say, Winnie Ruth Judd. Fortunately, we came at the right time; the archives were open. Within forty-five minutes a helpful archivist found the files we were seeking. Not much was left: maybe an inch of paperwork. We paid for copies to take with us.

Robin seemed happier after the catharsis of learning Jax's true identity. She had been right about him. We would probably never learn more. Robin suggested that I give the dog tags to Amy Preston, the ATF supervisor; perhaps she could pass them onto Jax's family. I had forgotten about them, and the idea alarmed me. This was, after all, evidence in a homicide investigation that we both had knowingly concealed. Better to let it be. She hadn't argued.

But we talked a great deal those days, about ourselves, about history and art. She was a good companion. Our lives were complicated and yet simple. It felt as if we had been friends on a deep level for many years. Her presence eased the sting of not getting the ASU job, the gaping absence of Lindsey, and I didn't worry too much about the future. Robin downloaded Chalino Sanchez songs from iTunes and we listened to them. I went running with her, starting to get into the best shape I had been in for several years. We made several visits to the art museum and I felt centered enough to read Kennedy's book on the Depression and World War II. Light rail took us down to Portland's for cocktails made by Michelle, the owner. The outside world didn't hold its former menace.

We read the newspaper together. In addition to the news of the dreadful economy, the Legislature slashing everything from health care for children of the working poor to closing state parks, and the silly features written to make readers feel better, it contained several stories about the "cartel hit squad" arrested and facing charges. It didn't mention's the hit squad's alleged murder of ATF agent Jax Delgado, of course. The reporter and editors also seemed oblivious to the larger implications of the arrests. So did the millions living here. Tea Partiers protested outside the Capitol against taxes, immigrants, and the government. They were too ignorant to know Arizona wouldn't even exist as a habitable place without aggressive government action. Every day a new real-estate project slipped into foreclosure.

Robin and I pulled our small, contented world closer around us. I told her more stories about old Phoenix and learned about some of her adventures. I took her to the old cemetery just west of the Black Canyon Freeway, and, under the canopy of its old trees, we left flowers on the graves of my grandparents and the parents I never knew. We took the rough brush from the car—meant to wipe off snow—and used it to scrub the dust from the headstones. We sat in the grass, and she leaned her head on my shoulder. Lindsey called every four or five days and talked to each of us. She talked to Robin far longer. Our talks were unbearably light considering the deep-soul talks that had been our sustenance for years. What was she listening to? Carrie Newcomer, Heather Nova, and Dar Williams. What was she reading? Marcus Aurelius and Camus.

When Robin and I emerged from our research at the State Archives that day, it had been raining and a very faint rainbow was visible behind the downtown towers.

Lindsey loved rainbows. She seemed to bring them out. I had seen more Arizona rainbows since I had met her than I had seen in my entire life. She would call me to the window to watch them, where we lingered while she painted the scene with her words, her arm around my waist. The summer of her pregnancy, the monsoon season was poised to be the new strange normal. When I had been a boy, the summer rainstorms had come into the city regularly from mid-July through early September. The lightning and thunder were spectacular. The rain constituted the majority of the precious seven inches a year that made the Sonoran Desert lush and unique in all the world.

When I moved back, I found a metropolitan area that had become a 2,500-square-mile concrete block. The summers were becoming hotter and longer, and the monsoons strange and unpredictable. In this strange new normal—all that most of this city of newcomers knew—the big thunderheads stayed beyond the mountains, as if they were gods surveying the mess that man had made of their timeless Salt River Valley. And when the storms rolled in, they were often violent. One storm two years before had been so savage that it knocked the telephone poles on Third Avenue straight down and ripped off some roofs. The meteorologists talked about microbursts and the collision of the weather front with superheated concrete, especially in places like Sky Harbor airport. I thought about how those storm gods might be releasing their kindled anger.

But while last summer had been hot and scary with the broken gasoline line, the monsoons had been as before. In addition to the obligatory dust storms and dramatic nighttime lightning shows, several times a week we had gotten real rain. And real rainbows.

One afternoon I had come home early and found Lindsey and Robin together in the upstairs apartment. Lindsey stood at the window as the clouds moved away and the room lightened.

"Oh, my God," she said. "It's a double rainbow."

It was: twins soaring all the way through the boiling sky toward Camelback Mountain.

"It's a good sign," Robin said.

An hour later, Lindsey started bleeding.

What is the dark matter that controls our fates, that brings catastrophes upon us suddenly? We are fools to even consider it. And what of the losses that we can never fully purge, never grieve away? Never make right. Never atone for. Never even hold a funeral or let our friends know what has collapsed us. Our child was gone without ever having breathed this fated atmosphere, without even a name.

My wife was only saved from bleeding to death by a procedure that meant she could never have children of her own. It was just another moment on a planet of tragedies, but it was our tragedy, our world knocked off its axis, taking with it all the tomorrows we had so vainly believed in. Later, when she was awake, Lindsey had demanded to know what had happened to her child. That was how she phrased it, "my child." The doctor was not delicate: the fetus had been disposed of in the hospital incinerator. That was the way it was. Lindsey had nodded once and stared ahead dry-eyed.

I looked back on those three months with Lindsey as golden. But the complexion of the time was more complicated than that, as any historian would tell you, more shaded, nuanced. Someday when I could bear it, I might see it with greater clarity. We had grown closer together than ever, and yet mysteriously also drawn apart, as if making room for someone. Lindsey became very dependent on Robin, and now it was clear that having lost her job and facing the worst recession since the Depression, Robin embraced being needed. They denied that they were going shopping for baby things. "I don't want to jinx it," Lindsey said. The poetic watchfulness in her that had first so attracted me became something more. She worried. She was acutely aware of changes in her body, even as the doctor reassured her. A few days before the miscarriage, she had said, "Something doesn't feel right," and the doc reassured her again.

But she would never be set at ease. These were the first days when I had seen her grow suddenly angry with me over seemingly like small things. But, in her mind, nothing was small. Although the breach was quickly healed, this was a new side of my love. And me? I probably did a hundred things wrong. Maybe the worst, that day when she first saw the blood in her panties, was to say, like a towering ass, "I'm sure it's nothing."

Now I was lost in the past as the rainbow faded over the Chase Tower. Robin lightly touched my shoulder. "Just be with me in this moment, David."

I nodded and we started to walk to the car.

She said, "It's all we really have."

Chapter Twenty

We carried the copied case files home and laid them out on the big desk in the study. I was tempted to give Robin the trial transcript, but didn't want her to get bored. She was excited by this historical sleuthing. So I divided the work, taking the transcript myself and giving her a small stack of police and arson reports.

It was tempting to look back on 1940 as a more innocent time, and that's probably true. Wars always change nations, coarsen them; Woodrow Wilson had known that on the eve of World War I. And the Arizona and America of 1940 had yet to go into World War II, much less the Cold War, and our current imperial adventures. Advanced communications consisted of dial telephones — the police radio system was only eight years old. Social networking was done at barber and beauty shops, the railroad depot, and the American Legion hall. But human nature persists in all its darkness, and even the little town of Phoenix had its share of violent crime back then. It also had a disproportionate amount of corruption.

The city commissioners themselves were said to control some of the local rackets. The Mafia was beginning to discover Phoenix, a town where cops and judges could be bought, where the banks could be used to launder money. On the outside, it was just a sunny farm town, surrounded by hundreds of thousands of acres of citrus groves and fields. My grandfather's dental practice was downtown. But Phoenix was also segregated, this place that had been settled by plenty of ex-Confederates. The relatively large black population, which came west with the cotton crop, went to separate schools. The Mexican-Americans were set off in their barrios. The main places everyone mingled were in the produce warehouses along the railroad tracks and in the red-light district on the east side. That was also the scene of Phoenix's worst race riot, when soldiers went on a rampage during World War II. The official death count was three, but probably was much higher. It was history the chamber of commerce didn't want you to know.

"Are you bored?"

"Yes." I was honest.

"It's fun to watch your face," she said. "See your mind wander."

"I just don't know how much we're going to be able to help Nick DeSimone clear his grandfather. I wonder why he even cares that much. I probably have several horse thieves and worse in my woodpile."

"You're just afraid of getting pulled into Peralta's orbit. Becoming a private dick." She said the two words with lewd glee. And it was true enough: I could see Peralta using this project as the "point of entry" drug to get me in his new game.

"What would be so bad about that?"

"I'm just tired of it."

"He's very entertaining," she said. "I remember the first time he said he wanted to tell me his philosophy. That's exactly what he said, 'my philosophy.' I was ready for something heavy and wise."

I quoted Peralta from rote: " 'If you find yourself in a fair fight, your tactics suck.' Don't get me wrong, Peralta probably saved my life when I came back to Phoenix. I really enjoyed the job. But I'm ready for something new."

"What?"

I just put my lips together and shook my head.

"There's no more market for history professors than there is for private art curators." Her face assumed a half-smile. "It wouldn't be bad. I'd work with you. We could make him fix that old neon sign."

"You're a dreamer," I said. "You could find work outside Phoenix."

"Do you want that?"

"No." I said it too fast.

"If you're done with the job, why did you bring home all those boxes of case files?"

"Maybe I'd write a book."

She gave me a disbelieving smile. "You were going to work those old cases. Admit it. I admire you for it."

"A few of them. I thought, in my spare time."

"That's the David Mapstone I know and love." She stopped and we looked at each other, not sure what to say next. Finally, she said, "For now, why don't we try to fight for Paolo? It doesn't sound like anybody did it when he was alive. This Harley Talbott sounds like a total creep, a big man with power. I know you want to be the objective historian, so I'll be the little cartoon creature on your shoulder, whispering in your ear, 'fight for Paolo.' It's a matter of simple justice."

"Fair enough."

I went back to the transcript.

"This is a funny name." Robin ran her fingers down one Xeroxed page. "Detective Navarre. Sounds like something out of a Bogart movie."

I slapped down the sheaf of papers. "You have got to be shitting me."

Frenchy Navarre. Sometimes it was spelled "Frenchie." I told Robin what I knew. He wore two guns and was one of the most brutal and dangerous cops the Phoenix force ever produced. If there had been a Bad Phoenix Cops blog in the forties, Frenchy would have generated a post a day. The worst Frenchy story was from 1944, when he was off-duty and given a ticket by another officer, one of the few African-Americans on the force, a man named David "Star" Johnson. Frenchy went into one of his rages, shot and killed Johnson right on Second and Jefferson streets. A jury acquitted him and he went back to work. Johnson's partner caught him at headquarters one day and shot him to death in revenge. The legend was that Frenchy went down shooting and the bullet holes remained in the stationhouse—then located in the old Courthouse—for years afterwards.

Now here was Frenchy Navarre as a detective on the DeSimone case.

Robin handed me the paper. It was a typed confession signed by Paolo DeSimone, given to Detective Navarre. Paolo said he was drunk and mad because Big Sam McNamara wouldn't sell him liquor. Later that night he came back with a can of gasoline and set fire to trash at the back of the building. I could imagine Frenchy beating the confession out of him. But that would be letting my prejudices get the better of me.

"The arson investigator's report." Robin held up two pages. "It says a firebomb was thrown through the front window of the store. That jibes with the newspaper accounts."

I looked it over and handed it back to her. The transcript was incomplete but raised questions, too. There was no public defender then. It appeared that DeSimone received legal counsel from a local lawyer either paid by the county or doing pro-bono work. He introduced several motions that were denied by the judge. One was to throw out the confession as coerced.

"You're onto something, History Shamus."

"Here's Navarre on the stand. He's asked why he arrested Paolo. Says he was given a tip by another man who had been in the drunk tank where Paolo spent the night on September 29th. Name of Eugene Costa. He told Frenchy that Paolo told him he burned down McNamara's."

I flipped through, trying to find if Costa had testified and what he had told Paolo's lawyer on cross-examination. The pages were missing.

"The joys of historic research: more questions than answers. All the cops and lawyers are long dead. I can try some of my retired police buddies, but they were too young. I don't see the hand of Harley Talbott in any of this. If he owned the judge and jury, we can't prove it."

"Don't give up." Robin went back to her half of the record.

◇◇◇

We kept at it for three days. The police records betrayed a slip-shod investigation. McNamara himself said he believed Talbott had ordered his store burned because he wouldn't pay the extra "taxes" demanded for Talbott's liquor. The cops never interviewed Talbott. The tip from Eugene Costa and the "confession" by Paolo kept them on a single, simple theory: one drunk Italian burned down the liquor store.

At the Arizona Room of the central library, we went through old city directories and phone books. Eugene Costa was listed from 1939 through 1948 and then he disappeared. Phoenix was a city of transients. I called around to the law firms to see if they had any information on the man who had defended Paolo—it was a long shot and came back empty. The fire department's arson records from 1940 were long gone. I couldn't find any manuscripts or diaries about Harley Talbott during this period. He had probably donated a fair amount to the library.

"So give me something else to do." Robin gathered up the legal pad on which she had been making notes. The Arizona Room hours had been cut back again and we were being told it was time to leave.

I admired her passion and persistence, saw something of myself in her. So I let her go down to the county offices to research land transactions from the period involving any of the principals we were tracking: Paolo, Talbott, Costa, Frenchy, the judges and lawyers involved. I would go home to Cypress where I would start to write a very incomplete report for Judson Lee. I would feel bad about taking his money. She kissed me goodbye beneath the shade screens of the light-rail station. She took the train south and I waited for the one heading north. I realized it would be the first time she was out of my sight since that last week in December.

Chapter Twenty-one

We worked together on the computer to finish the final report. We couldn't exonerate Paolo DeSimone. We could give a history of the case, from the initial firebombing to Paolo receiving a ten-year sentence and then being paroled after five years. The report also had background on Paolo working for Talbott as a driver and the power that the big man wielded in the city, as well as some of the allegations that dogged him past the grave. Most critically, we listed the investigative errors and inconsistencies, including Paolo wanting to take back his confession—given under duress to one of the most famously nasty cops in Phoenix history. Robin had added an appendix that painstakingly listed properties that Talbott owned in 1940, and some land bought by the otherwise mysterious Eugene Costa a few years later.

Judson Lee read quickly through the report, lingering on a few pages, and pronounced himself pleased. I told him not to bother with the money—I didn't believe we had earned it. In my old job, I had actually cleared cases. Peralta wouldn't have been satisfied with this. I handed the unsigned check back and said this was on the house.

"You don't give yourself enough credit, Dr. Mapstone," he said. "You know this city."

I thought about our recent travels into gangland. "I'm not sure anyone knows this city."

He scrawled his signature on the check with his small, sun-browned hand and passed it back. "Utter, ultimate, truth may be beyond the finest historian. This should be more than enough for my client to make a start to clear his grandfather's name."

I took the check. He shook my hand. Did his old-world kiss of Robin's hand and she laughed. I continued to apologize as he left, wishing we had found more, giving Robin credit for the good stuff. He waved it off, moving with surprising spryness.

"Anyway." He turned to face us on the front step. "Napoleon said, history was nothing but a fable agreed upon." Then he drove away in a new cream-colored Cadillac.

"It's five grand and nothing to sneeze at." Robin was reading the look on my face. "Let's go out and celebrate tonight." The smile took over her face. "I'll wear a skirt even."

I relented and felt my shoulders relax.

"You get to choose the place."

"Good. First, give me the keys to the Prelude."

I handed them over and asked her where she was going. It was an innocent enough question.

"Girl stuff." She walked out of the study laughing that wonderful, house-filling laugh.

A little after midnight Robin wanted to go outside and see the stars. We pulled on clothes and walked into the backyard, where the oleanders and citrus trees provided dark, sheltering masses around us. We sat in the old chairs by the chiminea that Grandfather had built so long ago. She lolled her head, sending her hair cascading down the chair back.

The vault of sky overhead had been degraded when they built the big freeway ten blocks south and by the pollution of four million people, but it was still clear and dark enough to make out the Big Dipper and dozens of companions. There was no moon and the scent of orange blossoms lingered for probably its last week this year.

"There's Polaris," she said. "Regulus…Arcturus."

I told her about my Boy Scout merit badge in astronomy, how I had forgotten nearly everything. How one year we came out at night and watched one of the Gemini capsules soar over us. This was before she was born.

"You must have been an adorable little boy."

"I felt like a freak." I smiled about it now. "Always had my head in a book. They made fun of me about my last name. I didn't have a mom and dad like the other children. My little friends always told me how ugly I was."

"I've seen the photos, David. You were a beautiful little boy." She laughed, the slight breeze carrying her big, happy sound. "Handsome, I should say. Adorable. I love those pictures of you."

She asked if I had played in this yard and I told her stories. We fought in the alley: oranges and dirt clods if the conflict was among friends, rocks if things got serious.

"Your own little street gang," she said.

We played in the yard. One year we spent the spring assembling discarded wood and building a boat that we intended to sail to India. I was nine and have no idea how the destination was chosen. But the map told us we could sail down the Salt River to the Gila, then into the Colorado and out into the sea at the Gulf of California. I was a child map nerd. The only catch was that the rivers here were dry, so we would have to wait for a flood. My grandparents were indulgent with our enterprise, even if the boat never touched water. Robin laughed and held my hand.

"So no play dates, no bus to school, no mini-van…"

"Nope," I said. "It seems like another country."

"It sounds like an idyll, even if your friends were mean to you."

"I learned to fight in seventh grade," I said. "So I owe 'em."

"I learned to fight, too," she said. "But not that way. I always envied the kids who could walk to school, live on a street with sidewalks, go to the same school for more than two years straight."

I squeezed her hand. "You turned out good."

We stayed out there for at least an hour, sometimes talking, often enjoying a communion of silence. The dull whoosh of the freeway and the occasional bell of a light-rail train were the only intrusions. The stars and planets seemed comfortingly fixed, whatever the reality of our orbiting world and expanding universe. A couple of airplanes circled toward Sky Harbor, but not one police chopper or siren disturbed our little universe.

"I've always loved the stars," she said. "Looking at infinity. Wondering why we're here, what's our purpose and destiny..."

Only for a few seconds did I imagine the child that might have survived to play in this yard just as I once did. I said, "We'll go to the desert sometime, get away from the city lights. It's incredible."

She pulled herself up and reached for me.

"Come on."

I stood and she stepped close, putting her arms around my waist. I tousled her hair and embraced her.

"You," she said with mock accusation in her voice. Then, "You have so surprised me. I didn't even like you at first, that day on the home tour when I came back into Lindsey's life. And you're thinking, who the hell is this? You didn't like me, either. Right?"

I tipped my head. "True enough."

That big smile remade her features. I had never seen her smile so. "Remember when I told you that it would be trouble if I got under your spell?" Her eyes were bright and merry. "Well, Dr. David Mapstone..."

She stopped herself, swallowed hard. My heart was very full at that moment and I said nothing.

"Come here." She pulled me close, nuzzled against me. "I want to tell you something."

"Your middle name?"

"Better than that."

I felt her warm breath, heard her whispers. Just a few words. I held her so tight, one arm around her waist, the other grasping her shoulders and back, feeling her body totally a part of mine.

Finally she whispered, "Are those happy tears?"

I held her away from me just enough to look at her and nod. I spoke her name and started to pull her close again. The next sounds were barely audible, more of an odd annoyance.

Thup...thup...

She bobbed sideways in my arms. Turning, I looked straight at a woman standing five feet away, no more. She held a pistol with a long silencer.

"Robin!"

She went heavy in my arms and I laid her gently on the grass. Her hair fell out around her face, which was already unnaturally pale. She stared at me, her eyes wide with shock. Her mouth was working words and nothing was coming out. Her left arm was bloody. More blood was coming out of her left side.

"Stay awake!" I yelled, barely conscious that the woman with the gun was gone. I screamed for help, kept calling her name, and held my hands behind her head, as if they could keep her from the ground. "Stay with me, Robin." I cried for help again.

She locked her eyes on me. I bent closer to see if she was breathing.

"David…" It was a hoarse whisper. Her eyelids fluttered and closed.

◇◇◇

The dispatch logs would show that the police and fire response times were within three minutes of the first neighbor's calls.

The first cops that came through the gate later told Peralta that they found me over Robin trying to resuscitate her, holding her, crying, and screaming. I don't remember the last part.

They told him that I was screaming, over and over, "Kill me!…Why didn't you kill me?!…" until they forcibly pulled me away from her body.

Part Three:
South Phoenix Rules

Chapter Twenty-two

I don't remember much of the next five days. The cops interviewed me and I described the shooter: an Anglo woman, short and slight build, with pale skin and stringy, long dark hair. She wore no makeup and her features were hard and life-beaten. I went through the PPD electronic mug book and found no one who looked like her. A police artist put together a composite sketch that was a reasonable likeness. Had I ever seen her before? No.

Lindsey flew home. We were careful with each other, as if handling delicate and explosive cargos. I said more than once, "I did my best." Every time I said it, I heard in my head a quotation attributed to Churchill: "Sometimes doing your best is not enough. You must do what is required."

Lindsey brought me two books from the Politics and Prose bookstore and didn't ask many questions. She didn't cry. Neither of us slept much. We both drank a great deal. She drank straight vodka as opposed to her old standby, a Beefeater gin martini. I avoided the newspaper. The day she flew out I drove back home to find a notice from the bank: Justin Lee's five-thousand-dollar check had bounced.

The telephone number on Justin Lee's business card had been disconnected. When I called Peralta, he said he didn't know the man aside from the day he came by specifically asking for me. I had let this snake into our garden. I noticed an unfinished pack of Gauloises left by Lindsey. I opened it, pulled out a cigarette and for the first time in my life lit one for myself. I smoked a second until I began to feel ill, and thought and thought.

In my old office, I had a white board on wheels. It was helpful in diagramming cases. Now I took a sheet of paper and tried to do the same thing.

I drew boxes and in them wrote "Sinaloa cartel" and "Gulf cartel" with a line linking them to the "Jesus Is Lord Pawn Shop." Another line branched off from the Gulf cartel to hold "Los Zetas." I set a separate "La Familia" box to the side, with no connecting line yet. Other boxes: "Jax," "ATF," "Barney," "hit woman." And at the top I drew a box and wrote "Judson Lee" until the pen nearly broke through the paper. I would have to find the connecting lines for all of them.

Peralta wanted to meet for breakfast, which was a problem. Our favorite, Susan's Diner, was closed, another victim of the recession. Peralta didn't want to go to the Good Egg at Park Central or Tom's Tavern downtown, where he would have to see all the politicos and make small talk. The line at Matt's Big Breakfast was too long. Linda's on Osborn didn't open that early. So we ended up at the Coco's on Seventh Street, where the place was almost empty and nobody noticed us.

"I'm going down to Casa Grande on a case," he said once we had placed our orders. "I want you to come with me."

"No."

He drank his coffee and we sat in silence until the food showed up.

"It's an interesting case. It could use your skills."

I had no skills.

He said, "You look like hell."

I didn't deny it. The omelet tasted vile, but that was no fault of the cook. I tried the Diet Coke, which tasted vile. Peralta reached into his suit-coat pocket and produced a leather wallet. He slid it over.

"Open it."

From years of following his commands, I involuntarily opened the thin wallet, revealing credentials for a licensed private investigator in the state of Arizona, issued by the Department of Public Safety. My photo and signature were on the card.

"Where did this come from?" Another forkful of the foul eggs and cheese. "No, no, don't tell me. It was in those papers I signed when I turned in my badge." I started to say he'd also made a claim on my firstborn, but stopped myself in time.

I left the wallet open on the table. Peralta munched scrambled eggs and bacon contentedly. "That other desk at the office? It's for you, Mapstone. I'll even buy you a bookshelf." He finished a piece of toast and let his coffee mug be refilled. "You have to let the police handle Robin's murder."

I stabbed at the omelet. The hash browns were no better. Everything tasted the same.

"The worst thing," he said, "is a hotdog. You were never a hotdog, Mapstone. Don't start now."

"What does PPD have?"

"Nothing. But they have a top team on it."

"Like you and Antonio?" I dropped the fork. "Nice job there. Los Zetas assassination team in jail. No problem, huh? Robin killed by an Anglo woman who looked like she stepped out of a trailer park. You guys deserve medals. I don't even believe these Mexicans you're holding killed Jax Delgado."

"You know this takes time."

"I don't have any more time."

"Come with me to Casa Grande. This is an interesting case."

"May I ask a question?"

He nodded.

"Is that Five-Seven licensed or registered?"

"Yes." He watched me evenly, which meant nothing with him. His dark eyes were angry, then alarmed.

I said, "That's too bad." I pulled it out and handed it back to him, no one noticing. I added the extra magazines of ammo to the tabletop, right by the ketchup and then I stood.

"Don't." That was all he said.

I started to leave. But I turned around and took the credentials, then walked out.

◇◇◇

For the next two days I had lunches that I couldn't afford at the Phoenician. The lush surroundings and spectacular view eluded me. I hated these people, the sharpies and phonies and wealthy vagrants that had ruined my city, that cared nothing for it except as a place to use up and throw away. The resort had been built by one of the archetypes: Charlie Keating. At least Harley Talbott had been home-grown trash.

No, I was there looking for the server who had called Lee such a charmer. If I was lucky, maybe I could charm her, even as I wondered if I was capable of a smile. She was off the first day, and I didn't even know her name. But she was my only potential link to him.

The second day was better.

She was not only working, but I was seated in her section without asking. I had trimmed up my beard and was wearing my best suit with a burgundy Canali tie.

"It's Mr. Lee's friend," she said, standing over me with a grin but no order book, this being a classy joint where the servers were expected to handle things from memory. "Where's your colleague?" Meaning Robin. I just let my internal bleeding go and smiled at her.

"He certainly likes you."

She raised her eyebrows and bobbed her head ironically.

I pushed a little deeper. "It looked like he'd been a regular for years."

"Oh, no," she said. "He's only been coming here for a few months. But he just has that way about him."

I agreed that he did and ordered lunch. That way about him: the harmless old guy, quick with a compliment and always wanting to know about her. As I waited for the food, I tried to figure out a shrewd way forward and kept coming up dry. Kept falling down into the places I was trying very hard to lay a thick concrete slab over just so I could move into the next sixty seconds of my life. I watched her graceful walk back toward the kitchen and wondered about her stake in this place. She was too old to be a high-school girl, and probably wasn't in college, either. If she were trolling for rich men the better job would be working the counters at Nordstrom in Scottsdale. Maybe she was a professional server in this tourist economy. Maybe she was an ATF agent.

Judson Lee. Attorney at law. Except that a call to a friend at Snell & Wilmer that morning taught me a few things. This veteran lawyer at the city's most prestigious firm had never heard of Lee. Nor was he listed in the Martindale-Hubbell directory going back more than twenty years. Just a charming old killer who had played me like a green rookie.

When it came time to pay the bill, I saw the server's name— Lisa—and told her it was beautiful. She smiled at me, but I was a few decades shy of being able to come off as the harmless old guy and my flirting skills were rusty. Oh, I wished that I still had my badge, which made it easy to ask questions, especially of citizens who want to do the right thing.

"Well, you tell Mr. Lee I said hello when you see him," she said. "I don't see him anymore."

"He's a busy man, Lisa. I'm sure he'll be in soon with another group of friends."

"Oh, you were special," she said. "He almost always dined alone." She paused, decided my Canali tie made me trustworthy, and went on. "I get the sense he's kind of lonely. Once he had a woman guest, but she seemed uncomfortable here, if you know what I mean."

"I do. Was this her?" I opened up the composite police sketch and slid it over so she could get a good look.

"Yes." Her voice was faint. "Am I in trouble?"

It was interesting to live in such an insecure-feeling America, where a man in a suit in possession of a piece of paper with official Phoenix Police logos on it had instant credibility. I asked her if she knew where I could find Judson Lee. Her eyes processed a response: Go get the manager? Say nothing? Risk losing my job if I don't cooperate?

"I swear, I don't know." She bit her lip, eyes heavily lidded. "I will tell you that he told me a story once. Kind of creeped me out, you know? How he had visited a strip club the night before. 'Gentleman's club,' he called it, but it was clear what he meant. Said he went there all the time. And he had to tell me the name, the Stuffed Beaver. Ick."

I folded up the composite and put it away, thanked Lisa, and signed the receipt. I gave her a big tip.

The Stuffed Beaver. It was the same place on Indian School Road where Barney the gun dealer had lost his glass eye in the stripper's stomach. At home, I drew a line from Judson Lee to the new box, the strip club, and another line that connected to Barney.

Chapter Twenty-three

The Stuffed Beaver sat in a building facing north on Indian School Road a little before 24th Street. It had been built recently as a Washington Mutual office, a typical ugly freestanding structure, then shut down by the mortgage bust and remodeled as a strip club. The name was proclaimed with a blazing blue-and-red sign, accompanied by a smiling cartoon creature that took up the entire street-facing facade. I wondered how it got past the city code. In smaller letters: "18 to cum, 21 to swallow." Wednesday was amateur's night. This was not amateur's night. The parking lot sat on the west side and extended behind the structure. Entry was through the back. That made surveillance problematic.

I couldn't go inside and hang around—both Barney and Lee knew me. While the parking lot was spacious, a man sitting alone in a car for hours might attract the attention of club security. Fortunately for me, the biggest beneficiary of Phoenix's bust was an outfit named "Available." Its signs were everywhere, including on the vacated older building directly west of the club. Behind it were five covered parking places with a direct view of the parking lot. I backed into one and waited.

My days were monsters, shooting me full of panic attacks that were only alleviated by trips to the shooting range. The nights saved me. The darkness covered me and made the city look less hideous, made me less aware of all that had been lost, the losses I carried around inside and ones that never occurred to the people who moved into a new "master planned community" on the fringes, only wanting the sunshine and cheap housing. Fewer were coming now. I had seen a story in the newspaper a few months ago that population growth might have even reversed. For seven decades, all Phoenix had to do was build houses and people came. Now the reliable old growth machine was flat busted. The "available" signs proliferated everywhere. The promising downtown condo towers were in foreclosure. The million-dollar faux Victorian condos on Central Avenue near my house were unfinished. Subdivisions rotted and were stripped of their building materials from Maricopa to Surprise.

For three nights I sat in my covered parking space, watching the men come and go. I had never understood the appeal: for me, sex was not a spectator sport. I saw the otherwise unremarkable young women walk through the parking lot wearing normal street clothes, carrying gym bags, heading to another night of work. Which one was named Destiny? I slowly worked my way through Lindsey's blue pack of Gauloises Blondes, trying not to see Robin's face hovering before my eyes. The club was open twenty-four hours, beyond my ability to cover. Considering the Jesus Is Lord Pawn Shop closed at six p.m., I decided to watch from six-thirty to eleven.

On the first night, I got a call back from Nick DeSimone, the Scottsdale chef. He told me things that didn't surprise me. He had never heard of Judson Lee. He had no roots in Phoenix and both his grandfathers had died peacefully in Chicago. I thanked him, hung up, and for the thousandth time cursed my naiveté.

All that time Barney never appeared, but after ten on the third night a familiar cream Caddy zipped into the back lot and parked in a handicapped space. Judson Lee got out and strode inside. Following him, quick-stepping to keep up, was a tall Anglo man, young, muscled, military haircut. He had a hawk's nose, as if begging for a pair of glasses, but there were no glasses. He was long-limbed and wide-hipped. The night was warm but he wore an oversized black windbreaker, just the kind of garment that might conceal a firearm.

I sat up straight in the car seat, a blend of rage and fear sending prickly signals through my legs. I unconsciously touched the butt of the Colt Python on my belt and ran my hand over the towel that covered the TEK 9, taken from the gang member who had been sitting on my street, resting on the passenger's seat. Its thirty-two-round magazine was full of nine-millimeter ammunition. I cursed Judson Lee aloud, my voice a strange companion in the silence of the dark parking nook. Another ten minutes passed before a Dodge Ram truck glided into the lot and Barney got out.

After six hours that the clock said were forty-five minutes, the three men came out again. Judson Lee and Barney talked animatedly, the slightly built lawyer gesticulating, Barney nodding and nodding. They seemed like an unlikely pair. Then Lee walked to his Caddy, turned to say one more thing to Barney, and got in the car. The man who looked unmistakably like a bodyguard drove. I started the Prelude and slowly slipped down the driveway with the lights off. When the Cadillac turned east on Indian School, I followed, letting a car get between us, maintaining a quarter-mile distance.

This was the point where the old David, so valued by everyone in my life for good judgment, would have called the police. Called Peralta. But the idea never occurred to me. The prickliness was gone from my legs. I felt comfortably frosty.

They turned south on Thirty-second Street and accelerated to fifty. The speed limit was thirty-five, but nobody in Phoenix paid attention to such niceties, so I was able to keep up and still blend in with the moderate traffic. That's what I told myself.

Much of this had been groves when I was little—Phoenicians drove out the two-lane roads and bought oranges and grapefruits from little stands—then it had been remade into middle-class, single-family ranch houses. Now it was going down, miles and miles. The well-off Anglos called it the "Sonoran Biltmore" and laughed. To me it was a haunted landscape.

The Caddy made the light at Osborn. Then it turned hard red. I cursed, made a quick right, a U-turn that barely missed an oncoming Chevy, then swung south again on 32nd and soon caught up, a safe quarter mile between me and Lee's taillights.

They caught the Red Mountain Freeway and sped east, all the way across the Salt River, past downtown Tempe with its new, derelict forty-story condo tower and the In-N-Out Burger at Rural Road, then swung south onto the Price Freeway, running fast now that the four-hour rush hour was over. Of course, this, too, had once been wide-open agricultural land. Most of it was built up in the years I was away from Phoenix and I barely knew it now. Knowing it didn't take genius: wide avenues every mile lined by the entrances to newer subdivisions of curvilinear streets and houses with tile roofs. Shopping strips anchored by a Fry's or Safeway sat on the major corners, along with huge gas stations. There were far fewer payday loan stores. The tableaux passed with numbing regularity. Better-off white families, the better-funded schools; the Intel semiconductor plants that provided a dash of diversity in the region's economy. Totally car-dependent. Except for the proliferation of brand-new Mormon and evangelical churches, this land was Maryvale half a century ago and didn't know it. I wondered how many of the husbands of the East Valley had stopped at a strip club on the way home.

I was four cars behind them at the red light for Chandler Boulevard when the feeling first bobbed against me. I set it aside when the light changed. Couldn't lose them now; wishing I could get close enough to make out the license tag. We whipped across the overpass and drove east again. Then the Caddy signaled left and entered a subdivision. I slowed down and waited, then followed them in with my lights off. The place was damnably well-lit, but I risked it, staying with the red tail-lights as they went straight, made a gentle curve, then a hard right turn onto another street. I approached the street at five miles per hour, nosing just enough beyond the edge of a house to see a large garage door opening in the middle of the block and the Cadillac disappear inside. The door came down.

It was a pleasant block, if suburbia was your thing. Yet it had all the charm of an empty cereal box. Newer houses were jammed together with postage-stamp lawns, wide driveways, three-car garages, and walled-in back yards. The entrances were small because the developer expected people to come and go through the garages. Those varied little more than the two or three styles of stucco tract houses, all painted to a palette ruthlessly enforced by the homeowners association. This was a place where people were supposed to blend in. If I had looked away for a second, I couldn't have recalled which house they had entered. But I didn't lose that second. I turned on the headlights and drove by at a normal speed, noting the address. Lights were on inside. No other vehicles were visible on the street.

But the feeling was still there: that cop's sixth sense that I was proud to have acquired despite my itinerant law-enforcement career. It was the awareness of being followed.

Chapter Twenty-four

It felt good to be back in the center city and I stopped at the taco truck on McDowell Road, in a dark parking lot a few blocks from the hospital. Even though it was nearly midnight, I had to wait in line to order two Mexican hot dogs. The music of Chalino Sanchez, or somebody who wanted to sound like him, was playing from portable speakers. The air was still and moody.

I sat in one of the lawn chairs opened on the pavement and for the first time in days actually tasted the food. A beer would have been nice, but I had to settle for a Diet Coke. They were fixed just right, cooked until the dog and bacon were one and covered in beans, tomatoes, and onions, to which I had added a few more goodies from the salsa bar. I ate the food and in my mind chewed over the meeting between Lee and Barney. Everyone was speaking Spanish but they took no notice of the Anglo in their midst. These were working people. They kept the local economy going and the whites from the Midwest hated them. I expected an immigrant sweep at any moment from the new sheriff.

Instead, a new Mercedes parked at my feet and a black cowboy climbed out.

He didn't walk to the order window. With a scraping on the asphalt, he moved a cheap chair next to mine and sat down. I was in the middle of the second dog and just let him be. The Python was in easy reach, and if he were packing, it would be in an ankle holster, so I could beat him to the draw. I didn't want any of that to happen. I just wanted to enjoy my hotdog.

"Nice evening."

I agreed with him. The man was around my age, with a thick neck and big hands. He wore jeans, boots, Western-cut shirt, and a white Stetson. The real Old West had plenty of African-American cowboys. You just didn't see them around 21st century Phoenix.

"Now I ran your tag through NCIC and the car came back clean."

I just wanted to live with the hot dog for one more minute. After the last swallow, I sipped the Coke and leaned back, watching the traffic. So who the hell was he? ATF? Phoenix cop? Chandler P.D., maybe, if my instinct had been right and he had been behind me for a while. No. He wasn't a local on the job. Otherwise, he'd have his badge on his belt and a firearm. Too flamboyant to be a fed. Could he be in Lee's employ and yet have access to the NCIC to check wants and warrants outstanding? I doubted it.

"So I had to ask myself," he said. "Who would be driving this old civilian vehicle and following my person of interest?"

"I'm a Maricopa County deputy sheriff." The lie came fluently. "Who the hell are you?"

"Then let's see a badge."

I rolled up the messy foil wrapping and wiped my hands. "I'm too goddamned tired."

He sighed. "Motherfucker. I get this close and the goddamned cops are trying to claim my prize."

Bounty hunter. But who was he after?

"We cooperate with bounty hunters all the time." Another lie. "Maybe we can work something out. Tell me why you're after the old man?"

"Old man?" The cowboy shook his head. "I'm after that felonious ditch pig who's with him most of the time."

"The big guy. Former military?"

"Dishonorable discharge. What matters to me is that he skipped out on a two-hundred-thousand-dollar bond in Bakersfield. But I spent twenty years on the force there before I became a fugitive recovery agent." And he obviously had buddies there still who would run my car as a favor to an ex-cop. He reached into his pants pocket and unfolded a piece of paper.

I looked at the wanted poster for Tom Holden, age thirty-two, and a face that went with Justin Lee's bodyguard. He had made bail on charge of aggravated assault.

"Bad actor," the cowboy said. "Considered armed and dangerous."

"How is he with a sniper's rifle?"

"Let me put it this way. He went to the Army sniper school at Fort Benning. I'm going to get something to eat."

He walked over and ordered while I studied the sheet. Tom Holden, another box on my chart, connected to Lee. If he had been the one who killed the La Fam members...

The cowboy came back, quickly downed a Mexican hot dog, and tilted his hat back on his head. He folded his arms and stretched out his legs, boot tips pointing into the night sky.

"I want to take him back," he said. "The problem is getting him alone. He's always with the old man. I can deal with that but it might get messy. A lot of the time he's with this crew of white boys that comes and goes from that house. Tonight I thought you were one of them, following the old coot for protection."

I nodded and asked him if he knew the old man's identity. He shook his head. I showed him the sketch of the woman who shot Robin and he had never seen her. His eyes were on the ten percent or more of the forfeited bond that he could make if he nailed Holden.

"I can help you," I said. "But you've got to book him into our jail."

"No fucking way, man. I'm driving him back to California. No muss, no fuss, no extradition hearing."

"Your subject might be wanted on a multiple homicide here." I let that sink in before continuing. "The case is coming together. You don't want to get in the way of that. You can work it out with your bondsman, make your money."

He wiped his mouth, sucked at his teeth, and thought about it.

"All right."

"There's one other thing. When you get him in custody, I want you to have him make a call to the old man before he gets to jail." I told him what Holden should say, word for word. "Can you persuade him to do that?"

He nodded. "I'm a persuasive kind of guy."

He reached in his pocket and produced a silver business-card case, handed me a card. Demetrius Smith, fugitive recovery agent. I pulled one of my old MCSO cards out and gave it to him. "Call me on my cell when you're ready to make a move." I wasn't really worried about him calling the landlines. With the way the county worked, it would be another three months before they were disconnected or reassigned.

I dreaded the house but there was finally no other place to go. The house that held so much of my past and had been our sanctuary amid all the troubles of the misbegotten city was now cursed. Why hadn't I taken Robin to Peralta's—maybe they could have tracked her there, too, but maybe not. Why didn't I get in the car with Robin and just drive. Drive east and show up in D.C. and let Lindsey deal with us. Drive west and find whatever it was that had propelled people to go west for centuries and did still. My god, the bed was huge and cursed. All around me, dark house, slamming heartbeat, the sensations of the edge of death, but no release.

Then the gunshots started and the bedroom glass shattered. I swear I could feel the bullets zipping just above the top of my body, which seemed to want to levitate up until a round found me. I slid sideways and dropped painfully off onto the floor, then took the chance of reaching up to get the Python. How many shots? I lost count at ten. A framed poster from the Willo Home Tour shattered as the far wall absorbed the bullets. I knew the next move: come through the front door. It was a shame I was on the near-side of the mattress, closest to entry to the bedroom, and with nothing to shield me. Then the shooting stopped. In the silence, I heard something hit the windowsill and clatter away. It sounded like a full can of soda.

The explosion put me flat on the floor.

I stayed there, smelling the sulfurous chemicals. I was a little dizzy and couldn't hear. The pistol stayed in my hand, my aim at the interior of the house. Then the ringing in my ears slowly receded and I heard the sirens.

Chapter Twenty-five

Kate Vare had been to the hairdresser, who had given her tint an even more lurid red. It looked like the interior of an active volcano. Her temperament was similar.

"You're holding back, Mapstone. I've been doing this for twenty-five years and I can tell. And you're a lousy liar."

"I'm the victim here."

"Sure."

We sat in an interrogation room of Phoenix Police Headquarters. The room smelled of urine and disinfectant. I had been taken there after the Fire Department had put out the small blaze in front of the bedroom window and a dozen police vehicles had sat along the street, lights reflecting off the houses. The responding uniforms and the initial detective team had been courteous. When Vare showed up, she ordered them to put me in handcuffs and take me out to a squad car. My rights were read to me.

"Do you want a lawyer?" Her lips suppressed a smile. Her leather portfolio was open but she hadn't made any notes on the empty yellow legal pad.

"Maybe I can use yours." Now uncuffed, I folded my arms.

"That goddamned blog." She muttered, then she leaned into me. "Let's go through it again. Your movements over the past twenty-four hours." So I did, giving the same sanitized version that I had used for the past two hours.

"You're holding back. You're a lying sack of shit. Your house was shot-up with an automatic weapon and a hand-grenade almost made it through the window. That's a gang hit. It makes me wonder what you've been doing to provoke it."

"Like the 'gang hit' that killed Robin? How'd that theory work out for you? I never heard of La Familia using an Anglo hit woman."

In this case, however, I wondered if she must be right. After all, I had survived the assassination of four top La Fam guys. We hadn't even been shot at. Word gets around. Now somebody was coming for me. I wished that I had the Five-Seven.

"Are you depressed, David?" Her eyes aimed toward the wall and I swear she started to tear up. "Lost your job. Your wife has left you. Your sister-in-law has been killed. Must be a lot to bear…"

I'd seen the view from the other side of the table enough times that I didn't give her so much as a blink of the eye. My facial muscles remained relaxed.

"Maybe you should get help," Vare said. "I hear Pristiq is effective."

It was amazing to live in our therapeutic and pharmaceutical society. How many great works of art seeking to transcend the tragic nature of life, how many majestic, melancholy personalities would have been lost to civilization if cave men had invented antidepressants and self-help books.

"Are you depressed, Kate?"

"You depress me." Her eyes met mine and her tone was harder. "You're a wuss. Weak. You always thought you could use that Ph.D to be some kind of United Nations observer of police work instead of getting your hands dirty. You got the publicity when cases were solved but I never bought it. You never fooled me."

Why did she hate me with such virulence? It was something I would have to answer another day. I said, "Then you know I'm telling the truth now."

She picked up her pen and made notes for at least five minutes, covering the writing from my view with her other hand.

She was probably making a grocery list; that's what I would have done. Just slow things down and make the suspect uncomfortable. Then she closed the portfolio.

"So you and Ms. Bryson were close? You were hysterical at the scene, I heard."

I just watched her.

"Maybe you had feelings for her? Wife's left you. Why, I don't know. Not that I'm asking. Her sister's right there. Wow. What were you capable of, depressed…weak? She struck me the same way. Oh, well, acts have consequences. There's this territory called adult that not everybody can enter. Where you can throw away your vows. Lie to the police."

I fought to keep my facial muscles neutral. "What are you doing to find out who killed Robin? She's dead because of you."

"Don't you dare," she said. "This is all your fault. Your stubbornness. Your stupidity."

That was fair enough. I said nothing.

"I read her autopsy."

All of my insides wanted to be outside. My temples throbbed concealing it. Vare watched me closely. The room vibrated silence for at least five minutes before she went on.

"You've got a concealed carry permit and a P.I license. I swear to god, Mapstone, if you're hotdogging this case, I'll do everything I can to see that you do time. Peralta can't help you. Nobody can. You're on your own."

That was true enough, too. But I was pissed. "You're either incompetent or you're holding back, Kate. It's one or the other. Which one is it?"

Her eyes betrayed surprise.

"I guess incompetent." Two beats later. "That, plus they're keeping you out of the loop because you'll be facing a grand jury. Ain't case management a bitch?"

She slapped her portfolio closed.

"God, I wish I had enough to hold you." She stormed to the door and turned back. "It won't take me long to get it." Then, to someone outside, "Cut the son-of-a-bitch loose."

◇◇◇

A sympathetic uniform gave me a ride home, where I found that a neighbor had cut a piece of plywood and placed it over the bedroom window. Aside from the eighty-year-old glass lost and the bullet holes in the bedroom wall, the main casualty of the overnight mayhem had been a mature myrtle planted years ago by Lindsey, now dead by hand grenade. The area below the window was black and some of the stucco had been blown off.

My cell rang. It was Demetrius Smith.

"How fast can you be here? I think we can get him."

I could get there in fifteen minutes, the freeways running lighter thanks to the recession. I met him in the parking lot of a shopping center near the grandly named Chandler Crossing Estates, which was just more suburban schlock no matter the moniker. I found the Mercedes and climbed inside.

"They're in there, grocery shopping."

"They must have good taste and lots of money." It was an A.J.'s, the upscale food store in town. Its parent company, the last locally owned grocer in Arizona, was in bankruptcy reorganization.

I noticed he appreciated firepower: a .44 magnum Colt Anaconda with a six-inch barrel sat underneath his sport coat. It was the big brother of my Python.

"He's only got one of these kids with him. So we ought to be able to take him. But don't take anything for granted, Mapstone. He's dangerous. Hell, these young ones today are dangerous."

And here they came, thankfully macho, grocery bags in both hands, paper not plastic. They walked toward a Kia, purple with black-tinted windows. We got out and made as if we were walking toward the store. We were one parking row away and they didn't even notice as we passed them, then we quickly cut over and came up behind them.

"Freeze." I said it in a conversational voice, my hand on the butt of the Python but the weapon in the holster. Tom Holden turned his head, betraying high, wind-burned cheekbones and cold, light-blue eyes. He tossed a sack at me but that was the oldest move in the world, one you learn as a young deputy serv-ing warrants. I sidestepped it, moved quickly to his side and put a foot behind his leg before I pushed him backwards. He fell hard to the pavement and expensive victuals fell all around him.

Smith stood over him with the long-barreled .44 magnum. It's a very unpleasant view for someone on the receiving end. Holden didn't move.

"Hello, Tom." His voice carried an amiable lilt. "Susie's Bail Bonds sends her greetings." He swiveled the barrel toward the teenager, whose face was pasty with fear between two grocery sacks. "Kid, if you even move, I'll blow your guts all over this parking lot."

I heard a murmur behind me. A pair of elderly women was watching us. I pulled the wallet and flashed my P.I credentials. "Maricopa County sheriff's deputy. Stand back, please." They complied. To Smith, in a lower voice, "get moving."

"I know my job." He already had Holden on his stomach handcuffed. Smith removed a semi-automatic from the thug's waistband, then painfully lifted him off the ground by his bound hands and marched him toward the Benz.

"Remember our deal."

He gave a little wave.

I was using the car keys that had spilled out of Holden's hand to check the trunk. I found what I had hoped for. "I'll give this young man a ride home." I ordered the teenager to walk to the Prelude carrying the grocery bags. It didn't look as if he was armed but you never knew.

Once he was in the passenger seat, I used an old pair of cuffs that Lindsey kept in the glove box to shackle his hands behind him, locked the door, walked around to my side, and drove. The entire operation had taken maybe three minutes.

"Where are we going?"

I ignored him and got out of the parking lot fast, then crossed the freeway into Phoenix jurisdiction, just in case the old ladies weren't so trusting of counterfeit authority. If Chandler P.D. rolled in, my move across the city limits would complicate things.

The downside: I was in the Ahwatukee district, or All-White-Tukee as the cops and firefighters called it, the world's biggest cul-de-sac with only three ways in and out, all from the east.

"Am I under arrest?"

I didn't answer. He was tall and skinny with a dusting of acne on his nose, the barest stubble on his chin, and curly brown hair. Just an all-American boy.

"I'm only sixteen."

I found another shuttered Washington Mutual branch and swung behind it. There was nothing but empty parking lot and a side view of the South Mountains over red-tile-roofs. Turning to him, I took his wallet and gave him a more complete pat-down.

"Hey, don't do that. I'm straight, so don't think I'm gonna suck your cock or anything."

Dr. Johnson said, "Nothing so focuses a man's mind as the knowledge that he is to hang at dawn." Lacking a rope, I had to use the tools at my disposal. My hand went gently behind his head and slammed it violently into the dashboard, which had been hardened by years of exposure to the Arizona sun. He was handcuffed and his abdominal muscles didn't even put up token resistance to the sudden forward movement.

"Ahhhhhhhhheeeeee!"

Blood came out of his nose but he otherwise looked fine except for a vague, terrible comprehension in his eyes.

Still, he put up a brave front. "Do you know who my dad is? You're out of a job, asshole."

"I don't give a fuck." I bounced his face into the dashboard again, harder this time, provoking another wail. Now he was bawling.

"Son," I began, momentarily taken back by the word. I had never used it before in my life to refer to someone. "We're going to have a conversation, and you have a choice. Either answer me honestly or I'll beat the shit out of you, literally. You people wanted a tough new sheriff. Now you've got him. If you get blood on my car, I'll shoot you and plant a gun on your dead ass. See what daddy thinks about his little junior then."

He sniffed hard and painfully.

"What's the old man's name?"

"Fuck you!" It was said more from surprise than bravado. "I'll get killed."

I reached for his head again to continue to build rapport with the suspect.

"Okay, okay. Sal Moretti. His name's Sal Moretti."

Something fired inside my brain. "Sal 'the Bug' Moretti?"

"That's right, motherfucker." He was still weepy. "Now you're gonna get yours."

"That dashboard really likes your face." I banged him into it again with slightly less force, but with all his pain centers running on high I might as well have thrown him off an overpass.

"Please! Arrrrrrrwwwwwwwwwwwwwwwwwwwggggggg…"

"What the fuck is Sal the Bug doing in Chandler?"

"Witness relocation. But he got bored playing golf. He's a real-time gangster."

"What a little honor student," I said. "Now ace the test. What…is…he…doing…here?"

His wet eyes were now full of fear at having his perfect nose irrevocably vandalized. "Black tar heroin, dog. He's got a hell of a connection. We sell it around to the high schools. What the fuck? There's ten of us. He picked us all by hand. All our parents have money and they're bored shitless with their lives. They don't give a fuck what we do. Anyway, we're all straight-A students, go to church, that shit. Cops ain't gonna bother us." He sniffed his bloody nose, making a disgusting sound. "You haven't even read me my rights. I'm a juvenile. My dad's gonna sue the county for a hundred million dollars…"

I moved my hand and he shut up. "I can drive an hour and there's a hell of a lot of desert where they'll never find your body. And if they do, they'll just think you're another illegal who died coming *norte*. The animals out there eat everything but your bones. You'll be just another wetback buried in an unmarked county grave." My voice wasn't hard; more of a reverie, which sounded scarier, even to me.

He was crying hard by this time. "What do you want?"

"Why did you follow us that night, outside the Sonic on McDowell?"

"Mr. Moretti wanted us to cruise by your house at night, just check on things. We saw you leave. So we waited near the Sonic. Tom wanted to do you both. Not, me, dog, I was scared, honest to god, I didn't want to be involved in a killing. But two of the older guys had guns, too."

"What stopped you?"

"Mr. Moretti. Tom called him and he said to chill."

"Where does the black tar come from?"

"Tom said the Sinaloa cartel."

"Oh, bullshit. Washed-up Chicago gangster and some teenagers who can't get dates running heroin for the Sinaloa cartel…"

"Real shit, dude! The demand is unbelievable. I'm making so fucking much money and that's just me. All I have to do is make some deliveries every week. Why should the fucking spics make all the money? Mr. Moretti's a legend and a real American."

I could have told him that Italians had once been held in the contempt now shown Hispanic immigrants, but what was the point? I asked him what Moretti supplied to the cartel in return?

"Money, lots of money." He puffed up his chest. "And guns. I've never seen so goddamned many guns."

"Where does he get them?"

"They don't tell me. Really, I swear to god."

I pulled out the image of the hit woman and held it in front of his rapidly swelling face.

"Who is this?"

"Sabrina."

He said it too easily to be dissembling. I wanted her last name.

"I think it's Cobb. Talk about a skank."

"What's her connection to Moretti?"

He said he didn't know.

"Then how do you know her?"

"I took a package to her, okay?"

"Heroin?"

"She'd a rather had that," said this straight-A product of what passed for the well-funded suburban schools. "But it wasn't." He tried to smile but it hurt too much. "I checked it, 'cause my ass would have been on the line, you know? It was ten thousand dollars. Hundreds and twenties. I made her count it, too, so she couldn't say I'd stolen anything."

I reached into the back and pulled out my old metal clipboard, which I'd carried as a uniformed deputy and had to dig out again when Peralta put everybody on standby for uniform duty because of budget cuts. Pulling his driver's license out of his wallet, I started writing up an incident report. It was mostly for show. The kid's name was Jonathan Zachary Grady. I wrote down his name, date of birth, address. He kept sniffling and suppressing his bawling.

"You're in a shitload of trouble, Jonathan."

"They call me Zack."

"I don't give a fuck. Are you following me?"

"Yes, sir."

"The old man is under surveillance as of an hour ago. I'm going to temporarily let you go because you cooperated. Do you skateboard?"

"What?"

His head crashed into the unyielding sun-baked polymer surface once again, hard this time. Blood spattered like July Fourth fireworks. He screamed.

"Yes, yes, goddamn, yes, I skateboard. Please don't hurt me!"

"Then it's too bad you fell off your skateboard," I said. "Don't go back to the old man's house. You'll go to jail and you'll be tried as an adult, then you'll go to prison. I'll make sure the prison gangs know you were a snitch, and by the time they finish passing your virgin asshole around…"

Out of his rapidly swollen face, he looked at me with growing terror.

"Don't go back to Moretti's house. Don't contact him. All his phones are tapped. Don't say anything to your buddies. We're watching them, too. This is a big case for the feds and they don't give a shit who your parents are."

He tried to nod vigorously but it hurt too much. He kept saying "yes" until I told him to shut up.

I ordered him to lean forward and unlocked the handcuffs. They had left no cuts or bruises on his wrists. He put a wad of McDonald's paper napkins I gave him up to his nose.

"Now get the fuck out and walk. And thank you for your cooperation."

Chapter Twenty-six

I used surface streets to return home. The stop-and-go gave me time to assess new information. Sal "the Bug" Moretti—Judson Lee—in Chandler, comfortably relocated thanks to our tax dollars, and now running new criminal enterprises. Selling black-tar heroin to affluent high-school kids. Somehow involved with the Jesus Is Lord Pawn Shop, selling guns to the cartels. This was what had showed up on our doorstep, peddling himself as an attorney with a bogus story.

Why? What was his role in the beheading of Jax Delgado? The answer ate at my insides all along the length of Baseline Road, as I passed the cheap, fake Tuscan-Spanish architecture of apartments and subdivisions, profaning the land that once held the Japanese gardens whose images so enchanted Robin. He wanted to get close to Robin. Maybe he had wanted to see how effective our defenses were. Maybe…I didn't know.

I had let this happen.

Beyond that, it was all little things. Holden wanted to kill us that night, but Moretti had held him back? Why? Had Tom Holden been the long-rifle shooter who had taken down La Fam as we watched stupefied? What was the Bug's angle in that killing? I cursed so long, loud, and profanely that I fogged the inside of my sunglasses.

The drive gave me time to assess new information about me. The packets of wet wipes Lindsey kept in the glove box did an adequate job of cleaning the blood off the inside of the car and my hands. But I had seen my own capacity back there with Jonathan Zachary Grady, middle-class teen drug dealer. I had enjoyed it, this darkness that had been growing in me suddenly let out into the sunlight. I kept wiping my hands long after the little cloths were dry, kept wiping them until my skin was raw.

On Central, I turned north, crossed the canal, passed Sue's Fashions, and took in the brown cloud hovering over the skyline. In the historic districts, everything was blooming and lovely. This was the garden city of my youth, the green oasis, what was left of it anyway. It was lost on me. I was almost home when the cell rang. It was Peralta. This time I picked up.

"How's Casa Grande?"

"Why aren't you answering your phone?"

"I've needed quiet time."

"You're a really crappy liar. I heard about the gunfire at your house. You need to get out of there. Come see me and gun-up."

"No."

The line was silent for several seconds. "Do you still have the wallet you took off the banger watching your house?"

I hesitated.

"Because he's a DEA agent," Peralta said.

It was eighty-five outside but I felt chill.

He continued, "Don't start on me. I just found out myself. So don't fuck this up. Bring me the wallet and the TEK-9."

"I don't have a…"

"Crappy liar, Mapstone. I need the gun back before Amy Preston sends me to Guantánamo or you murder somebody with it."

"Fine. Fuck you. What was a DEA agent doing watching our house before I ever got in the middle of their investigation?"

He had already hung up. That answer, of course, was obvious: their man, Jax Delgado, had been killed and his head sent to the Spanish revival house on Cypress Street.

The next call came two hours later.

"Mapstone, it's Demetrius. Thanks for your help back there. You have good moves. I hope you got the misguided lad home safely."

"Where are you?"

"Sorry, my man, but I just crossed the state line. Ditch pig will be safely in jail in Bakersfield when you need him, and I'll be thirty-thousand-dollars closer to paying my daughter's tuition at UCLA."

I just let the microwaves carry silence until he said my name again.

"Did you make him do the phone call?"

"He did it just the way you wanted. Sorry about the rest, but California called."

I put up a fuss, made it a good one. But I was satisfied. Demetrius Smith had not let me down.

Now I sat in the living room and looked around the house. "Just get me to the night." I said it over and over, as if it would stop the tachycardia that was overwhelming me. The only thing that helped for a few moments was to lie in bed, where the sheets still had Robin's scent.

◇◇◇

The address the high-school kid gave me went to an old, single-story row of apartments on 15th Avenue north of Missouri. This part of the city had developed slowly, the cursed subdivisions creeping in on the acreages and farms. Some properties still had horse privileges in the zoning code. But I was not going to horse country. The apartment was in the middle, behind a fading white door that had no peephole in it. There was no back exit and the lights were on. It was full dark.

I walked through the smell of citrus blossoms that only fed my blood lust and gave the hollow-sounding door three knocks.

"Who is it?" A female voice.

"FedEx."

The door cracked and I pushed through, raising the barrel of the Python to her face.

"Oh, shit!"

She turned to run and I grabbed her by her hair, smashed her into the wall, and dragged her inside, kicking the door shut behind me.

"Who else is in the apartment?"

"Nobody"

I told her we'd double check. With her hair pulled painfully and the big Colt against her back, I made her do a walk-through, to the bedroom, the bathroom, the closet. Then I pushed her back into the living room and threw her to the floor.

It was the same woman: thin, pallid face, long dark hair, wearing dark shorts and a teal top. In the light, she looked about five feet tall. She stared up at me with terror. In the light, her face was prematurely crisscrossed with lines and her skin carried the unhealthy pallor of an addict. I sat in a chair and kept the gun on her.

"Why?"

"Oh, mister, please, I'm begging…"

"I'm going to ask again." My voice was quiet, unfamiliar. "Why?"

"He said he'd pay me, okay? My old man's in jail and I was trying to get him out."

"How did you find him?"

"He found me, I swear to god."

"Who found you?"

"Mister Lee!"

So he had played the same game. She didn't know who he was or where he lived. She might have been the woman who had lunched with him at the Phoenician, who, recounted the server Lisa, felt out of place.

"My old man had done some work for him before. When Mister Lee called here I was desperate to raise that bail money. There was nothing I could do and I asked for his help. He said I had to do this."

"Why?"

"He said you'd shot and killed his son, that both of you were drug dealers, and he wanted justice."

"Why didn't you shoot me?"

She stared at the wall. "The gun jammed."

"Where is it?"

"Under the sofa cushion. He said he'd pick it up. But that kid who brought the money wouldn't take it."

I told her to get the gun, hold it by the barrel, and put it on the coffee table. She pulled up a black .22 semi-auto with a silencer attached to the barrel and set it next to a stack of "Real Simple" magazines. I ordered her to lie back down on the floor.

"Did you bail out your husband?"

She shook her head.

"Where's the goddamned money!"

Her eyes grew wide. She pointed to a black satchel sitting against the giant flat-screen television set.

"You didn't smoke it?"

"No, no! I've been thinking about leaving, starting over. Donnie beat me anyway, so I thought, maybe this was my shot. Let him stay in jail." She held bony hands against her face. "I know I did a bad thing. I know I did wrong. All I ever did before was turn a few tricks. I was in jail for that but nothing else. I swear to god, mister. I wasn't raised…"

She suddenly stopped talking when I held up my hand.

"Do you have a dishrag?"

I had to repeat myself.

She nodded and pointed to the kitchen. It was wet and draped over the 1960s-era faucet. I picked it up and tossed it to her.

"Put it in your mouth."

She hesitated until I cocked the Python. The move is not necessary in a double-action revolver, but the sound gets attention. "Please, Mister…" I aimed. She started to eat the dirty rag, tears running down her cheeks. She lay on the floor, raised on her elbows, staring at the madman over her. I replayed that night in the back yard, Robin hit and falling. I felt shrapnel rubbing up against my heart.

I holstered the Python and pulled out the latex gloves from my pocket. I slid one on each hand and then examined the .22. The magazine still had ammunition. I worked the action to make sure it wouldn't jam and slapped the ammo back into the gun.

"I know you've studied your Northern Ireland history," I said. "The Irish Republican Army used to do something called 'a six pack.' A bullet in each ankle, knee, and elbow. You'll probably live, if you can stand the pain, and you don't bleed out. I don't care."

Here I was lying, because I intended to put the last bullet between her eyes. Muffled words. Steady streams of water coming down her face.

"You killed an innocent woman. You didn't kill me. Two strikes and you're out." I hefted the cheap, poisonous manufacture in my gloved hand.

My cell rang. I made the mistake of looking at the caller I.D.: Lindsey.

Inside the Lincoln Memorial, where he sits in his chair watching what has become of the republic he did what was required to preserve, words are carved into the walls. Among them,

> In this temple
> As in the hearts of the people
> For whom he saved the union
> The memory of Abraham Lincoln
> Is enshrined forever

The inscription never fails to move me. But as Lindsey and I stood there that night, barely noticing the light crowd around us, I began to weep full-out.

We had walked the length of the mall. I had been once again trying to coax a talk about the natural disaster that had befallen us. Lindsey, once again, had been silent. None of this was new, nor was my inability to leave it alone. Inside, I tried to imagine the events of grievance, misunderstanding, and disregard that, beyond losing the baby, were pulling her away from me. It was a fool's errand, of course, worse than asking for trouble. I didn't understand why we had to mourn separately, or why we couldn't talk any more. Once again, I suggested that we try counseling, together or separately.

At this she had turned to me and nearly snarled, "I don't even know who I am!" before stalking ahead.

It had become clear that the distance separating us was one that couldn't be crossed with an airplane ride. How we had gone so far off course, little by little, was probably beyond either of us that night.

And I cried there before the engraved words, not knowing how to save my union. She wasn't wearing gloves and put the hand without the wedding rings on my arm.

"Dave, I don't know how to tell you…" Her voice was nearly a whisper. "The last thing I want to do is add to your sorrows or be cruel to you…."

"Just say it, Lindsey." My gut tightened.

She said, "I'm not sure I want to be married to you."

Now I let her call go to voice mail. The woman was imploring me with wide eyes, a shaking head, and making small, animal-like sounds through the dishrag.

My left hand pulled back the action and chambered a round. I would start with her kneecap, supposedly the most painful wound. Her right kneecap that was two feet away. I slipped my finger inside the trigger guard, lined up the sights, and took a breath, started to let it out slowly. This moment had been imagined in my sleepless nights and days a hundred times, T.S. Eliot hammering in my brain, "After such knowledge, what forgiveness?"

But that moment I heard Lindsey. And I heard Robin. Voices as clear and insistent as if they were sitting next to me. They would not let me be.

I put the gun on the table and walked out into the cool night.

On the sidewalk, I called PPD and told them I had just seen the woman who had murdered Robin walk into an apartment. The first units showed up in three minutes. I could clearly identify her and would have great credibility on the witness stand as a decorated former deputy sheriff. The murder weapon and money were there as evidence. I would take my chances with the justice system I had spent so many years serving. This time.

Chapter Twenty-seven

The next night I drove toward the blinking red lights of mountaintop communications towers again. Something kept drawing me back to south Phoenix and I didn't know what it was.

When I was a boy, our weekend drives to the Japanese gardens were down Seventh Avenue. Often we stopped at Union Station along the way so I could watch the passenger trains, or see the freight cars switched across the many tracks—seventeen as I recall—that crossed the street at grade level. Now Seventh Avenue soared across the tracks on a concrete overpass, but it didn't matter because Union Station was closed, the passenger trains were gone, the thriving industries that once lined the tracks were empty lots or decaying buildings, and most of the tracks were long gone.

Back then, we drove through the poor side "south of the tracks." No bridge carried cars on Seventh Avenue over the Salt in those days—we simply followed the pavement across the dry, wandering riverbed. One of the many quarries was near the road and it contained a pit nearly always filled with water. I imagined it as a fathomless depth, and for a child from a place with dry rivers, even passing close to this tiny inland sea filled me with terror. The city gradually fell away, replaced by pastures, fields, groves, and irrigation ditches, presided over by the South Mountains and the Sierra Estrella. I hiked both of them as a boy and from their summits, the green fields, this civilizing enterprise, which went back centuries to the Hohokam, only barely kept the desert wilderness in check. The wild West and the frontier seemed very near.

Almost all this was gone as I drove south now. Seventh was a wide arterial with curbs and sidewalks. It crossed the river on a span with no character or beauty, matching the built environment of the entire route. If the tree restoration along the river was moving this far, I couldn't see it. The quarries had moved farther west and the river had been confined to an unnatural dredged passage to prevent flooding. I saw one old farmhouse and a rickety barn that transported me back to being ten years old. But it didn't last. When I hit Baseline Road, I turned east on just another look-alike, six-lane Phoenix highway, known locally as a "street." The agriculture, and of course, the flower fields with their fantastic spectrum of colors, were long gone.

If you followed the road in the opposite direction, it led to a spot that marked the Gila and Salt River "baseline" for the surveys of the territory and the state. It was one of the most important manifestations of the white man's conquest of the land. In many ways, it was the beginning of everything you saw now. Hardly anyone knew about it. The only way you might get their attention would be to say that the baseline is near Phoenix International Raceway, but you wouldn't keep their attention long. This wasn't their hometown. They had come here to escape history.

But history would not be evaded long. Perhaps that's why I kept coming down here. South Phoenix had always been the poor side of town. The barrios and shantytowns near Buckeye Road and Seventh Avenue were slums so atrocious that they were identified as some of the nation's worst during the Depression, this when Phoenix was smaller than a hundred other cities. Much of the area lacked even running water or a sewage system. This was where Father Emmett McLoughlin toiled for decades to help the poor, and the Henson housing project was built in 1941 as a beacon of hope—not the crime-infested danger zone I later knew as a young deputy.

Now an ugly new apartment complex had replaced even that, a good intention I was sure, but the trees and shade that had once made Henson livable had been torn out, swapped for gravel and off-the-shelf suburban architecture. The old black community had diminished and although the Hispanic population had soared, the barrios had been disrupted and in many cases destroyed.

The Anglos who ran Phoenix historically thrived on ignoring the south side—prospered through its cheap labor, kept comfortable in their soft apartheid. It was a place to put the landfill, the toxic disposal outfits, and all manner of not-in-my-backyard enterprises. It was a place whose history was to be overlooked and marginalized. Now I wondered how much had changed, despite the newer subdivisions along Baseline, the tilt-up warehouses that were raised on spec, or the city signs that proclaimed this "South Mountain Village."

The well-off had decamped for north Scottsdale, Paradise Valley, and the fringes, leaving millions of working poor all over the city that once haughtily neglected these neighborhoods. Every place outside of the newer areas was partly south Phoenix now. But this place, south of the tracks and, especially, south of the river, was also special, anointed by its unique history, and it had soul and edge, however many cheap, new houses sat behind walls along Baseline, no matter how horrid the fast-food boxes that squatted at Central and Baseline.

I turned north, the city lights briefly before me, before I crossed the canal, passed the Catholic church, and started the long, slow glide back to the valley's center. The gaudy lights at the Rancho Grande supermarket were misleading. No place had been hit harder by the combination of the recession and the anti-Hispanic fervor of the Anglos than South Phoenix. The Ed Pastor Transit Center was nearly deserted, with only one bus idling in the bays. A man filled large jugs from a water machine while his children yelled from the open windows of the car. Did the water machines mean the families didn't have operable plumbing? For whatever reason, they proliferated here.

It was this reverie that prevented me from noticing the vehicles that swarmed me.

They executed the maneuver as expertly as cops handling a felony stop. We were just south of the Central Avenue bridge. I was boxed in by a tricked-out Honda in front, a white car behind, and, what finally got my attention, a jacked-up, extended cab pickup truck. Before I could fully react, the truck swung over and bumped the Prelude into a warehouse parking lot. Then the car ahead suddenly stopped, forcing me to brake hard. I had the insane thought: Was this where the old Riverside Ballroom stood? I had a choice between using the cell to dial 911 or pulling out the Python. I chose the latter. But by then, six men were on the far side of the car, M-4 assault rifles with scopes and laser sights leveled at the windshield and door. All wore black protective vests.

Oh, I wished I had the Five-Seven. I wished I had backup. I wished Robin's laughter still graced the world and that my wife loved me and that our child would have lived a long and full life and remembered us well. Instead I had six rounds in the Python and two Speedloaders. Eighteen rounds in all, but no time to reload. The Prelude was not, to put it mildly, armored. More men appeared around me, but they evidenced no gang hauteur. Instead all moved with a military-like competence. If this wasn't the ATF, I had only one hope. It had little chance of success, but it was all I had.

South Phoenix Rules.

I was not afraid as they tore open the driver's door and dragged me out, taking the Python, pinioning my arms at my sides, and roughly backing me up against the side of the car. My spine bent painfully backwards. The men all spoke Spanish. They were not the ATF.

"Let him go."

This command came in accented English, his voice sandpapery. My arms were released.

A dark-skinned man walked close. He was my height with bad skin and dressed all in black, including a Kevlar vest. Now I really missed the Five-Seven. He spat in my face.

"You gunned down my people and you just thought it would be okay?"

"I didn't have anything to do with that."

"Why did you do it?"

"I didn't do it. Didn't you read the newspaper?" Of course, he didn't.

"Screw this. Take him." My brief and conditional freedom was rescinded, replaced by strong hands gripping my arms.

"You were lucky last night. We should have just come in the house and finished it. But this will be better. I'm going to feed you to my dogs. They like human flesh. They have a taste for it now. But first, I want you to have a little traveling companion. Let's say it'll help keep you quiet."

He produced something dark and round, and another man latched onto my head.

"Open his mouth! Pull on his jaw!"

The next few seconds passed in a long, painful, frantic dream-state, ending with a man's scream, something like a wet Chicken McNugget in my mouth, and half-proprietorship in a hand grenade.

A man was still screaming, as well he should. I had just bitten off one of his fingers at the second knuckle. Now I spat the bloody remnant on the pavement and stared at the *jefe*. The idea had been to put the grenade in my mouth. He held it up to my face as I struggled. Unfortunately, the man's timing was bad and I have good teeth. The sudden turnabout had caused four-finger's friends to loosen their grip, and I latched onto the grenade.

The *jefe* held it too, trying to wrestle it from me, tendons standing out in his neck and forearms. The crew could easily have overpowered me, but everyone hesitated. They could see that I had control of the top and the pin. That provided enough time to bend forward and pull the pin with my teeth.

Then I spat it away. The metal hitting the pavement was unnaturally loud.

The leader tried to back away but I wouldn't let him. I held his hands wrapped in mine. His men were unsure what to do. The man who now had four fingers on one hand was reduced to moans as he ripped off his shirt to staunch the bleeding. All were confused by the new reality that had entered their lives: South Phoenix Rules—when you're outnumbered and backup can't arrive in time, when you have more assholes than bullets, all you can do is become the crazy Anglo.

I spat bloody saliva back at him. "Let's all die today."

His eyes widened and he tried again to disengage. It didn't work. I had one hand firmly around his grip on the grenade and my other hand as the only thing holding down the safety handle. If my left hand was pried away, it was nearly impossible that anyone could move fast enough to keep the handle from springing, setting off the fuse, and leading to a short-countdown to explosion. What was it? Five seconds? Was it worth the risk? All had come to realize that *el gabacho loco* held their destiny, literally, in his hand.

I went on in Spanglish: "*Ya no se puede hacer nada. Estamos jodidos.*"

They all knew there was nothing they could do. We were screwed.

"Who the fuck are you? La Familia? No, too disciplined. Los Zetas? Mexican police? I don't even give a shit." I lightly fluttered my grip atop the safety handle and everyone tensed. Four Fingers stopped whimpering.

"You..." The leader stammered as his men regained themselves and aimed their M-4s at me. A new sheet of sandpaper colored his words. "You're not going to just walk away..."

"Then we're all gonna meet God in five seconds, and even if you shoot me, I guarantee you'll go with me when this *piña* blows." I watched his luminous brown eyes as they failed to blink. My arms ached but I fought to conceal it. "Or, we can talk, *entre machos*, warrior to warrior. "

"What can you possibly give me?" he demanded, his hand still firmly in my grip. We were both sweating heavily but his hands were starting to shake.

"I can give you what you want."

Chapter Twenty-eight

Back at the house, I tried to take stock. After brushing my teeth like a maniac, I put the Bill Evans Trio on the sound system, made a martini, and settled at the desk to think. I thought about Lindsey, wondered about the man or men she might be seeing. Might be in bed with right now. What was he like? Lindsey was so conservative, almost a prude in some ways. Now I guessed she had rubber to burn. My lodestar lost, perhaps irrevocably. Common male jealousy twined with my vivid imagination wrestled with grief over control of my emotions and lost. The level of the liquid in the martini glass went down. I was too broad shouldered to carry off the narrow neckties popular when Bill Evans was at his peak. I still didn't understand why Robin mattered so much to Sal Moretti that he would put a hit on her.

For the first time, I looked at Robin's legal pad as more than a painful relic. I pulled it over and started reading the notes she had made on that long afternoon she spent alone, after she had given me a kiss at the light rail station near the central library. Soon, I was making my own notes on a separate pad.

Peralta answered on the second ring.

"Have you murdered anyone?"

"No."

"And you just happened to see the hit woman walking down the street several miles from your house."

"I was just a concerned citizen." When he didn't answer, I went on. "You still have the contacts to get a fast-track check on military records…"

He reluctantly said yes.

I read him the information from the aged dog tags that I held in my hand.

Then I called a friend back east. She was an expert in the history of the Mafia. It was late her time, but she was indulgent. Something in my voice, perhaps. When I ended the call, all I could do was lay my head on the desk.

The next morning, I was at the ASU Hayden Library early. The Arizona Historical Foundation archives were a starting point at least, and by ten, a preservationist named Susan had set me up at a table where I was surrounded by the comforting mass of gray Hollinger boxes.

The Japanese internment of World War II was one of the sorrier chapters in American history, when more than 100,000 Japanese-Americans and Japanese living in the country were forcibly moved from the West Coast into concentration camps. The reasoning had been fear of a Japanese invasion or sabotage of war industries, even though there was never an instance of sedition or espionage. But it had been arbitrary: Hardly any Japanese living in Hawaii, which had actually been attacked, were interned.

No matter: the anti-Japanese feelings that had long simmered, especially in California, were unleashed by Pearl Harbor. Franklin Roosevelt signed executive order 9066 in 1942. Many were brought to camps constructed in Arizona, including one at Poston, in the western desert. Most lost everything and after the war had to start over. Today, conservatives were defending this move by the otherwise hated FDR as a useful precedent for profiling Muslims living in America. Everything comes around.

At my crowded table, like a credible historian, I moved through primary source material, the recollections and documentation of people who had actually been there. The Frances and Mary Montgomery Collection—they had been teachers at the Gila relocation camp south of Phoenix. The Wade Head Collection—he had been the director of the Colorado River War Relocation Center at Poston. I set aside the memoranda about camp construction and organization. Letters about individuals and families took more of my time.

It was a rich archive. I wanted to spend a month there and listen to the hours of oral histories. There was no time. And I couldn't find much on the relocation in Phoenix itself. It was probably there. Everything is somewhere, if you look long enough—ask the archeologists who found ancient Jericho. But the records concerning Arizona related to the camps themselves. The same was true of the secondary source materials, such as the scholarly articles and a couple of Ph.D. dissertations.

I was ashamed to know so little. I remember Grandmother telling me about the German prisoners of war being marched into town to work. About the Japanese, she and grandfather said little. I did remember one thing: the line that separated the families to be relocated from those who could stay ran along U.S. Highway 60—Van Buren Street and Grand Avenue. Those living south of the boundary, including the Japanese farmers along Baseline Road, were sent to the camps.

I found a couple of good academic articles, but they were mostly confined to Japanese immigrants to Phoenix and Maricopa County prior to World War II. First-generation, or Issei, families began arriving early in the 20th century. The first American-born child came around 1906. The state's Alien Land Law of 1921 prohibited property ownership by "Orientals," but it was overturned in 1935. The Japanese were innovative farmers and encountered prejudice and envy, but they also built good relationships with many Caucasian farmers and business owners. Kajuio Kishiyama was among the first farmers near the South Mountains, first leasing land and then buying it. Members of the Nakagawa family were also early growers. Both had been interned during the war. After the war, they came back and started over.

With these flimsy threads, I tried to narrow my search.

Peralta called at one. He had the information that I needed.

Back home, I pulled out phone books, opened up Google on the Mac, and started making calls. It was tedious work but at least it kept the panic attacks away. On the thirty-seventh try, I reached a man who took my name and number, and said he would talk to his cousin. In an hour, a young woman called. After some persuading, she said she would be willing to talk with me. She lived near Los Angeles and agreed to meet me the next day.

I made another call, to a cell phone I was sure couldn't be traced, not that I even wanted to try.

"I need another forty-eight hours."

"I knew you'd fuck me over." The sandpaper voice. "I should have killed you when I had the chance."

"It didn't work out that way."

"Maybe you're afraid to get your hands dirty, history teacher."

"You know better than that."

"Why should I even trust you? You're a former cop?"

"Because you want more than me."

He didn't speak for a long time. Then, "I'll give you twenty-four. That's all. Then we're coming for you, this time for keeps. We'll start by cutting off your finger."

"Whatever."

I flew into Burbank and rented a car, driving an hour through the dismal traffic to a comfortable house with a view of the San Gabriel Mountains. It was not a very smoggy day. Phoenicians always talk about not wanting to become "another L.A." It's the smugness of yokels. Phoenix had become another L.A. in all the bad ways, including the gangs. It lacked almost all the good things, from the extensive rail transit to the cool vibe to the world-class universities and talent. Oh, and there was the ocean—and mountains, when you could see them, as magnificent as the San Gabriels.

The young woman I had spoken to on the phone only had a youthful voice. She was close to my age, but attractive with shoulder-length hair, large eyes, and a fine figure in an expensive suit. It turned out that she worked in the L.A. County District Attorney's Office and was not prepared for any bullshit from David Mapstone, of late the historian for the Maricopa County Sheriff.

"I checked you out," she said, standing in the doorway.

"Did I pass?"

My flirting skills still needed work. She said, "Let me see them."

I handed her the plastic bag with the dog tags. She took them out, held them in the sunlight, and ran a finger over the metal.

"Oh, my God."

She introduced herself as Christine Tanaka Holmes, stepped aside, and let me come in.

She led me back into a large family room lighted by an arcadia door that led out onto a sumptuous garden. But much of the interior space was taken up with the tools of old age: a walker, a four-footed cane, a wheelchair with a thick, black cushion as the seat. And in a print armchair sat a small, very elderly woman with hair the color of lead pulled back into a bun. She assessed me with bright eyes.

The deputy D.A. bent down on her haunches.

"GiGi, this is David Mapstone from Phoenix. This is my great-grandmother, Sarah Kurita. GiGi, he brought Johnny's dog tags home."

I pulled up another chair and sat before her as she held the objects. Tears dimmed the bright eyes. She took both of my hands. "My big brother, Johnny."

She instructed the younger woman. "Bring them."

We sat in silence, her diminutive, bony hands clutching mine, until Christine returned. She opened a wooden box and began to hand out objects.

"This was Johnny in 1943. He sent it to us in Poston, from his training."

The photo showed a cocky smile on a young soldier. "He trained in Mississippi, if you can believe that," Christine said.

"He was his own man, Johnny," the old woman said. "He was a rebel, had to do it his way. Didn't want to follow the old ways. Wanted to marry who he wanted. He was such an American boy, even though they called him a Jap. But he was a good brother and a great soldier. He didn't want to stay in Poston. He and his friends enlisted as soon as they could. It wasn't easy. Lots of resentment about what the government did to us. But Johnny was going to show them."

More photos: Johnny with other soldiers; aboard a troop ship; another man. "This was his friend Shigeo," the old woman said. "He was killed on the beachhead at Salerno." She touched each of the photographs as if they were religious icons. "Johnny wrote us every other day." She pointed to stacks of letters inside the box, neatly tied with silk bands. "Johnny fought all the way up Italy and into France, with the rest of the 442nd." Her face clouded. "Then he came back home…"

Christine said quickly, "The 442nd Regimental Combat Team was made up exclusively of Nisei who chose to fight for their country. It was the most highly decorated unit in the Army's history—twenty-one Medal of Honor winners. Meanwhile, their relatives were forced to live in the relocation camps." She allowed her first smile. "But you know that."

Next came shadow boxes with medals and ribbons. One was a Silver Star. It was the third highest decoration for bravery and this one looked as if it had just come from the War Department. In a laminated cover was a citation for Johnny Kurita, for gallantry in action against the enemy at the battle of Biffontaine.

All this was living history, right before me. I let it wash me along, carry away my impatience, and then distract me from my heartbreaks and losses. Against all this, mine seemed small.

Two hours went by at warp-speed before I finally asked my questions. Her hearing was keen, so I could speak in a normal voice. Her memory was vivid and precise. The answers she gave knocked me sideways. The same was true for Christine.

"GiGi, I've never heard this before."

"What was the point? We knew we couldn't get justice in Phoenix. The other Japanese on Baseline tried to help us, but they were just getting re-established. Most of the whites didn't care. Oh, we grew so many things. The South Mountains shielded us from the frosts. The whites just said we were taking the best land. What was the point in carrying around such bitterness." She nodded to Christine. "None of you young ones knew. Except…well, he read Johnny's letters, so I eventually told him."

It was only then that GiGi wanted to know, so politely, how I had found Johnny's dog tags.

Chapter Twenty-nine

After the mandatory hassles at Sky Harbor, I was back in the Prelude by six that evening. The sunset was ordinary. As I took the exit out the east side of the airport, Peralta reached me.

"Where have you been?"

"Scholarship."

He silently weighed my answer. "We're taking down the Jesus Is Lord Pawn Shop. Want a front-row seat? You can sit in the command van with me and the A.G. Those guys you saw loading guns into the SUV? They work for Antonio. We've got probable cause. We've got the buy on tape, the fake paperwork. We've got enough now to shut down the new supply route. All the muckety-mucks from Washington signed off at last. So we're finally going in. It'll be fun to watch Barney frog-marched off to prison."

I told him no thanks.

"Why not?" It was a demand, not a question.

"I'm just trying to put all this out of my mind."

"Good luck," he said.

On the freeway south, I made another call. I had an obligation to repay and the clock was running against me.

The walnut with eyebrows opened the door himself. He stood, slight inside his loud golf shirt, blinking at me.

"May I help you?"

I just pushed my way past him. "Where are your punks?"

He stepped outside, did a careful check of the street. The only vehicle in sight was Lindsey's Honda Prelude. He turned back.

"I don't even know you. Why have you forced your way into my house?"

It was a good act and he kept it up in his old-man voice, even after he had produced the Beretta and begun a careful search of me, not just for a weapon but also for a wire. When he was satisfied, he used the gun barrel to prod me into the Arizona Room.

"Now, Dr. Mapstone, you have become an intruder on my property, so I can shoot you at will and be perfectly within Arizona law."

"But you're curious why I'm here."

"You do surprise me. Sit." He hospitably waved the pistol toward a leather sofa. The room was large, decorated at some expense but still vulgar: cowboy paintings, a bejeweled saddle on a stand, a grandfather clock encased in faux adobe, and gigantic leather furniture.

I dropped into the sofa and he gingerly sat across from me, his hips barely on the seat, as if he needed to be ready to spring up at any moment.

We seemed alone, but I asked again about his teenage henchmen.

"Back home for dinner with their families. I wouldn't want them falling in with the wrong crowd."

"And what a mentor they've found. Salvatore "Sal the Bug" Moretti."

He cocked his head in mirth.

"If we had the time, I'd love to know how you found me."

Part of my brain sized up that angle: He didn't know that I had followed him from the Stuffed Beaver. The honor student I interrogated with the dashboard: I told him Moretti's house was under surveillance and his phones were tapped; if he went back or warned Sal, he'd be arrested. Tom Holden had made the call I wanted—with the persuasion of Demetrius Smith—that a California bounty hunter was after him and he needed to lay low and not risk bringing the cops to Moretti's house. Too many days had passed, so Sal had assumed that his identity and location were secure. But he didn't strike me as someone who would be introspective in the face of the crisis now sitting on his leather sofa. As he said, if we had the time…

So I just said four words, the lethal information I had gained from my friend the organized crime historian.

"Eugene Costa, your grandfather."

One black eyebrow went up.

"He wasn't just a gofer for Harley Talbott," I said. "He was a middle-man between Talbott and the Chicago mob. The DeSimone case was bullshit, of course. But the articles mentioned Eugene Costa. Just a bit player. A nobody, unless you knew what you were looking for. Unfortunately…" My throat started to close and I slowed myself down. "Unfortunately, Robin happened to run Eugene Costa through some old property records and put that information as a footnote to the report we gave you."

"You're a genius." He aimed the gun at my chest.

"She didn't know anything. Neither did I."

"They always say that." His voice sounded thirty years younger and I could imagine the many executions he had carried out. In fact, I knew about ten of them. He must have negotiated a sweet deal with the feds to avoid the needle. If I were thirty days younger, I might have been afraid, might have been anxiously worried about time—just like that little boy at Kenilworth School, watching the clock. None of that was in my mind now. I settled in the sofa and spread my arms over the back, feeling the cool leather on my hands.

"You're an idiot," I said. "You rat out your old pals, get witness protection to resettle you here, and pretty soon you're selling black tar heroin to high-school kids. You can take the goombah out of the rackets but you can't take the rackets out of the goombah."

"I opted out of witness protection a year ago," he said. "They check in every now and again, but you know how it is, war on terror, budget cuts and all."

"You might have gotten away with it if you hadn't paid ten thousand dollars to that woman to kill Robin and me."

"It would have been twenty thousand if she'd done the job right. I should have had Tom do it."

"Like he did the job right on Jax Delgado."

He moved his finger off the trigger, curious.

"It was meant to look like La Familia's work," I said. "But because you'd seen Jax with Robin, you figured she was a risk, too. So you had Holden send her his head. That way, when she ended up dead, the cops would think it was another killing by Mexican gangs. Nobody would ever suspect you. So far so good? But you learned her brother-in-law was a deputy sheriff. You backed off. You're a careful guy. You wanted to know what Robin had learned from Jax: so you did the Judson Lee thing, gave us a cold case, quoted Napoleon on history. You provided us with just enough information that our findings would tell whether we knew the secret about Jax and you."

He moved the Beretta to his lap, watching me intently. I remained sprawled on the sofa.

"Robin didn't know anything." I spoke slowly, letting each word hit him. "She was just a thorough researcher. It got her killed." A voice in my head: *David, you got her killed.* I said, "You killed her and it made me curious why."

"I don't like curious guys."

"That's why you killed Jax, too. Too bad he was a federal agent."

Moretti opened his mouth but nothing happened except a string of saliva separated between his lips.

"Oh, you didn't know that, Sal? You thought he was El Verdugo and he'd go to work for you? Be some insurance against the cartels?"

"What the hell are you talking about? You're a crazy man!" He stood and backed away, keeping the gun on me. At a 1950s-style bar cart, he poured himself Scotch, neat. He didn't offer me anything. Slipping the gun in his pocket, he consumed two fingers of the booze in one gulp.

"Jax Delgado was ATF," I said. "He discovered that you were off the witness protection reservation. But it wasn't the heroin he was after. It was the Jesus Is Lord Pawn Shop, which you secretly own through your friend Barney."

The two black eyebrows slithered up his forehead. "Smart guy. How do you know this?"

"Just destiny."

He slapped the glass down hard and paced the large room. It was amazing how isolated the space felt, but it was designed to be that way, so people could come in their garages, watch television and play video games, and never notice what might be going on outside their front doors.

"Nobody can prove it!" His voice echoed into the high ceiling.

"I thought you old-school guys didn't kill cops, code of honor, and all that shit."

"It's no shit! It's real. This Mexican passed himself off as a contract killer. The best! I don't kill cops. Don't you realize I could have killed you and the girl anytime? I could have had you killed in that parking lot with those spics, but I didn't. I am a man of honor."

"Forgive me, Salvatore." I said it with the old-world flair of Judson Lee, and then laughed slow and low. I thought he'd shoot me right then, so I continued quickly.

"Johnny Kurita," I said. Moretti's tan dialed down by half. He slowly returned to his seat, gripping the gun. "Jax wasn't just here to take down your gun pipeline. He wanted you on personal business. It was the kind of personal business his bosses didn't know about: the murder of Kurita by your grandfather, Eugene Costa."

Now the pigments reversed: a stroke-red blush broke its way through the stony brown skin.

"Personal business? Now you're talking nonsense. What was I to him, huh?"

"You helped your grandfather in the killing."

That was just a wild pitch, an improvisation that suddenly came to me—I didn't have any evidence—but it found its way across the plate and he went for it.

He nodded very slowly and stared past me. "You do live up to your reputation, Mapstone." He idly stroked the pistol in his lap, trying to figure me out. The young Sal the Bug would have killed me by now. The man before me knew he was in trouble, knew there were now too many loose ends. He stood again, agitated, and for a moment I thought he would pull out his own box of mementos. Then he sat again and said what was logical: "How the hell do you know?"

"I talked to Johnny Kurita's little sister today."

He watched me in silence for long minutes. The grandfather clock chimed.

"They were both hotheads." Moretti was reliving the long-ago moment. "Grandfather and that Jap kid. They argued, then they fought each other right out there in the flower fields. I wasn't going to let that Jap disrespect my grandfather."

The black brows, the only trace of hair on his head, narrowed. "He came back from the war, this Kurita, and thought he was a real American, that the world owed him something. He wanted that land back. It wasn't his anymore! Japs couldn't even own land down there on Baseline for years, you know. Then they started coming in like locusts. When the government took the Kuritas' property during the war, we got it fair and square. Hell, we'd have even leased it back to them."

"You stole it. And Harley Talbott made it all look legal down at the courthouse."

His mouth crooked down. "So what? Talbott owed my grandfather. Talbott owed the Moretti side of the family back in Chicago. The Costa side, the heirs all became totally legit, and sold that land for millions in the nineties. Funny, we buried the Jap right behind the flower shed that night. Now he's under a parking lot by the swimming pool."

I didn't speak until he stopped laughing.

"What is history but a fable agreed upon, right?"

He was silent. The pistol drooped slightly in his hand.

Then, "None of this had to happen. I was minding my own business when this Jax, this man who you say was an agent, shows up at my home and starts asking questions about my grandfather Costa. He was a Mexican, for Christ's sake. Supposed to be a hit man, supposed to only go through Barney. How the hell did he even know where I live? How did he know what happened in 1947? He wasn't even born yet. The flower fields are a goddamned bunch of apartments now."

"Maybe he didn't even care about the land."

"What the hell would he care about?"

"Simple justice." I waited two beats. "Because Johnny Kurita was his great-grandfather."

A palsy ran down the left side of Moretti's face.

"Before he enlisted in the Army, Johnny met a pretty Mexican-American girl who was working at the Poston relocation camp. When he came home, he married her, and they had a baby boy. That little boy's grandson was Jax Delgado."

"And you've come here unarmed to tell me this? You have a death wish because I killed your sister-in-law?"

"Yes. What about you?"

"What the hell do you mean, 'What about me?'"

"Don Salvatoré, you've been double-dealing so long you don't even know right from left," I said. "Selling guns to Sinaloa, selling guns to the Gulf cartel, too. Having your buddy Tom assassinate four top La Familia men. Why? Because you were afraid of what they might tell us? Because you want to set one side against the other like back in Chicago? You think you'll profit from it. Well, you're not in Chicago anymore, asshole. You're playing way out of your league."

He raised the Beretta.

The front door crashed open.

Sal looked up, confused by the laser scopes dancing on his chest. He quickly put the gun on the table and smiled.

"This man tried to kill me, officers. Thank God you got here…"

The men I first encountered on Central Avenue moved with the same sinister efficiency. Sal was pulled up and handcuffed before he even comprehended what was happening. Then he saw the roll of duct tape. His panicked eyes met mine for a long ten seconds.

"Wait." I took the duct tape myself.

"Zack," I said. "The kid who delivered the money to Sabrina. Did he know what she was going to do to earn it?"

He squirmed in the grip of the men, staring hatefully at me. "You goddamned right he did. I gave him the chance to do the job himself, prove himself a man, but he was a little coward."

I wrapped the duct tape around his bony head myself, covering his mouth even as he tried to keep speaking. I shoved his pistol in my belt. Then the men hustled him out to a waiting SUV, its motor quietly running. Within two minutes, we were all gone from the pleasant street where everyone was deep inside the Arizona Rooms watching television and where bad things never happen.

Elegy

Low clouds hung over the city the night that Lindsey and I hopped the fence and made our way into the old cemetery. It was now called Greenwood Memory Lawn but it had been around since 1906 and was still adorned by hundreds of old trees shading the well-manicured grass. The city had grown around it and left it behind.

It was just as well. The news of local mayhem had been especially harrowing lately. It turned out that a Chicago mobster, Sal "the Bug" Moretti, who had been put in witness protection here, was selling heroin out of his Chandler house, using teenagers as couriers. The teens all came from "good families," and neighbors of Moretti were quoted: "these kinds of things just don't happen here."

Moretti was also the secret owner of a big gun shop on Bell Road that was raided by the feds for selling guns to the drug cartels. A decorated ATF agent had been killed as part of the operation, and Moretti would be charged with murder, too. If they found him. Although ten teenagers from Chandler and Ahwatukee had been arrested, Moretti had apparently escaped. "Vanished without a trace," the news stories kept saying.

Indeed.

Not every case was unsolved. In Bakersfield, a man already in jail was charged with the murder of four men in Maryvale the previous month. The police said a sniper rifle, found in an abandoned car, had linked the man to the killing. The case was broken thanks to an anonymous tip to the Silent Witness line. I checked the Web site for the Bakersfield paper and two days later learned that extradition wouldn't be an issue: Tom Holden had been stabbed to death by another inmate, who was reputedly a member of La Familia. Meanwhile, every day brought news of fresh death south of the border: fifty killed in one day. The cartels kept growing, alliances shifting and breaking apart, the organizations dividing like cancer cells.

But in Phoenix, after two days of careful excavation, the bones of a World War II Japanese-American veteran had been discovered under the parking lot of an apartment complex on Baseline. Kate Vare was in the newspaper saying it was being treated as a homicide from the late 1940s, and that the discovery was the result of "painstaking police work by the cold-case unit."

Indeed.

Now we walked past the tall old memorials to the familiar graves: my parents, my grandfather and grandmother. The flowers that Robin had left a few weeks ago were broken and dead. There was no room left in the family plot for me. We had bought a space for Robin in the garden columbarium. But I knew she wouldn't want that and Lindsey had agreed.

We brought her ashes with us and gently spread them across the family plot. It amazed me how little was left of a person. I fought the pressure building against my eyes and the tightness in my throat. Lindsey was already weeping. Ashes to ashes. Dust in this valley of dust. This valley of tears. Civilization was breaking down all around us. It had happened in Phoenix before, with the Hohokam, when things grew too complex and nature rebelled, human nature bowed and broke.

Now it was happening again. It was starting all over, right here, in this city that had risen from its ashes and was being devoured again, starting here and moving across an America that didn't even pay attention to Phoenix.

Civilizations fell.

I followed Zack Grady for an entire week. Sal Moretti's Beretta was tucked in my pants with a full magazine. The all-American drug dealer who took the cash to Sabrina, knowing she had killed Robin. He had been offered the job himself and turned it down. But he didn't go to the police. He didn't do anything to stop it. While wishing for sleep at night I ran the scenarios through my mind, how I would grab him, drive to a secluded spot in the desert, and put a bullet in his brain. I let Sabrina live. Something inside me felt sorry for her. Zack — in many ways he was the worst of the lot. He was a young sociopath who was just getting his first taste. The next time he would be happy to kill. He had been someone's adored child once, but that made me despise him even more. He had survived.

The last night I watched as he walked down a half-mile length of cars at Chandler Fashion Center, his stride full of insolence. The Prelude tracked him slowly from behind, lights off, the pistol gripped in my right hand. The passenger window was down and I would simply order him into the car. Maybe I'd handcuff him again. Or maybe I'd just beat him into unconsciousness with the police baton in the back seat.

I let him go. I was so far down a darkened path that I didn't know how I could find my way back, find my way back to Lindsey and some semblance of the life we once had, find my way to a future I could at least endure. Taking him into the desert would only push me further into the darkness. I had already found parts of myself that frightened me. We were the good guys. That was what Peralta always said. It's what separated us from the ones like Zack and Sal and Tom Holden. I let him go. Two days later he was arrested as one of Sal's dealers.

Inside the cemetery, Lindsey and I listened to the cars roaring on Black Canyon Freeway, the sirens on 27th Avenue, a quick succession of gunshots, the echoes of the Tea Party rallies at the capitol where the legislature was destroying what took a century to build here, the last cries of the immigrants dying of thirst in the desert. Who will excavate our ruins of Wal-Marts and parking lots? Who would want to?

But at that moment, sheltered by the big trees, the low clouds, and the enchanted Sonoran Desert twilight, we sat cross-legged on the grass and leaned into each other. When I was a child, I had dreaded the trips out here. Cemeteries had frightened me. Grandmother's love of the place had given me the creeps. Now I understood the matchless peace and beauty here.

"Poor Dave." Lindsey stroked my arm. "Nick and Nora Charles are fictional characters. You thought you were marrying this sweet young thing with cheerleader legs and with no history and we'd go out and make the world right."

I had never assumed that about her—well, maybe the cheerleader legs—but I said nothing, happy to hear her voice.

"You've taught me so much. Opened so much of the world to me. I love the jazz and martinis and cops. And the history… oh, Dave. You told me everything about yourself and your adventures, but you don't understand. For me, where my life wasn't dull, it was something I was ashamed of, something that made me feel worthless. I didn't really understand what has been building inside me because our being together was such a gift."

"All I ever wanted was you," I said. "And truth and bone, as you once said."

She laughed lightly. "Easier said than done, I guess."

I wanted to say that her history hadn't made her worthless. Far from it. But I wondered who she was now. She spoke first.

"Did you fall in love with Robin?"

In love. Such a loaded word, especially for women. I had grown to like, admire, and probably love Robin. If I lingered too long in that contemplation, it would be unbearable. I said, "I cared for her."

She put her arms around me. "You care too easily." That weightless laugh again, then a sob. "Robin built a lot of walls to protect herself. But I can tell you…"

She swallowed hard. "I can tell you, she cared for you right back."

The broken shards sitting against my vital organs again shifted painfully. When I could speak again, I said, "I'm in love with you. With you, Lindsey. I think I was from the first moment I saw you."

"I know."

Draw me a map of the human heart. I am lost.

"I've failed you so much, David. I lost our child. I failed Robin."

"No. Never."

"It's true. My life is a failure."

I stopped for a moment. A light rain baptized my forehead. "Turn off your Linda Unit, Lindsey Faith."

Now she laughed fully, my old Lindsey, if only for a moment.

Five minutes later I gathered the courage to ask, "Do you love him?"

"I don't think so," she said. No hesitation. After a long pause: "I just wanted to feel something again."

The shrapnel sliced against my heart. How long before I would just bleed to death?

I said, "You left me once before."

"I know."

And that was all she said. We were both damaged.

The rain was falling hard and straight now, seeping through our clothes. It felt fine. We watched as Robin's ashes vanished into the grass and the timeless soil.

"Oh, God." Lindsey choked it out.

We held each other and cried a long time in the precious spring rain. I prayed that we would all be together again in the morning. Then I helped her up and she kept her index finger in my hand as we walked together through the darkness, trying to find our way out again.

Peralta was tapping slowly on a laptop computer when I walked into his office the next afternoon. He looked up, unsurprised.

"You think you're real clever, don't you."

I shrugged.

"You could have gone to jail."

"I know."

"You could have been killed."

"That would have been fine."

"Have you ever considered…" He stopped, for he probably knew I had considered everything. My dirty hands were at my side, my academic detachment lost like luggage thrown out on a distant highway. I almost said: *maybe I've become more like you.* But I didn't say it because I didn't know what I was becoming. Whatever it was had no regrets over the rough justice meted out to Sal Moretti or Tom Holden. The detached part of me that remained knew it wasn't quite right. But if I looked too long in the rearview mirror this would be the least of the demons chasing me. Peralta leaned back, straining his luxurious executive chair.

I looked around the place. It was as homely as it was austere. But this was where he had decided to make his stand. And it occurred to me, amid all the madness, that he was my oldest friend. Lindsey didn't know what she wanted. Robin was gone. My hometown wasn't home any longer. But my oldest friend was here, making his stand. So I would make the stand, too. I desperately needed to make this stand. So I said I was ready to go to work.

"About goddamned time!" He barked it but his face radiated relief.

"Two conditions."

"Oh, fuck." He closed the laptop and opened his arms: hit me.

"First, I want a decent chair, like you have."

He nodded. "What else?"

"Restore the sign out front, neon and all."

"Do you know how much that would cost?"

I stood there with folded arms.

He mashed his lips together. Then: "Mapstone, you're a real bastard. All right, we'll do the goddamned sign. Now I'm in the historic fucking preservation business, and all to provide a welfare-to-work program for a washed-out professor who's a not-bad lawman…"

I let him keep talking as I settled behind the other desk.

Somewhere I heard Robin laughing.

Paying My Debts

Once again, I called upon my police brain trust, especially Cal Lash and Bill Richardson; as usual, they provided invaluable help. Frank "Paco" Marcell, retired from the Maricopa County Sheriff's Office and now running Crime Assessments LLC, is Arizona's leading expert on gangs. He was very generous with his time in guiding me through the labyrinthine passages of gang land. David William Foster, regents' professor at Arizona State University, Virginia Foster, professor emerita at Phoenix College, and Deputy Maricopa County Attorney David R. Foster assisted me with everything from the history of the city's barrios and cleaning up my rusty Spanglish, to keeping my firearms protocols straight. Talk about a family with talent. For help with the Japanese internment, I'm grateful to Jack August, Jr., research professor at the University of Arizona and the best historian in the state, as well as Emily Thompson of the University of Georgia. John Bouma of Snell & Wilmer, a great lawyer and a man of living history, aided me in recalling other pieces of old Phoenix. As usual, blame me for any errors, deliberate changes, or inconsistencies. Finally, as should be clear, America has a treasure in the independent Poisoned Pen Press, and my thanks go to Robert Rosenwald, Jessica Tribble, Nan Beams, Marilyn Pizzo, and Annette Rogers. Most of all, my editor Barbara Peters helped bring it on home with her customary skill and grace—without resorting to South Phoenix Rules.

To receive a free catalog of Poisoned Pen Press titles, please contact us in one of the following ways:

Phone: 1-800-421-3976
Facsimile: 1-480-949-1707
Email: info@poisonedpenpress.com
Website: www.poisonedpenpress.com

Poisoned Pen Press
6962 E. First Ave. Ste. 103
Scottsdale, AZ 85251